Roscommon County Library

LEABHARLANN C

D0513256

This book should be returned not la.
shown below. It may be renewed if not requested by ～～～～ ｜0۵

another borrower.

Books are on loan for 14 days from the date of issue.

F/LP

DATE DUE	DATE DUE	DATE DUE	DATE DUE
16. MAY 05.			

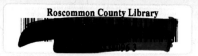

brothers get their comeuppance?

RODEO ROUND-UP

Roscommon County Library Service

**WITHDRAWN
FROM STOCK**

RODEO ROUND-UP

by

Curt Longbow

Dales Large Print Books
Long Preston, North Yorkshire,
BD23 4ND, England.

British Library Cataloguing in Publication Data.

Longbow, Curt
    Rodeo round-up.

    A catalogue record of this book is
available from the British Library

    ISBN   1-84262-355-9 pbk

First published in Great Britain 2004 by Robert Hale Limited

Copyright © Curt Longbow 2004

Cover illustration © Prieto by arrangement with
Norma Editorial S.A.

The right of Curt Longbow to be identified as the author of this
work has been asserted by him in accordance with the
Copyright, Designs and Patents Act, 1988

Published in Large Print 2005 by arrangement with
Robert Hale Ltd.

All Rights reserved. No part of this publication may be
reproduced, stored in a retrieval system, or transmitted in any
form or by any means, electronic, mechanical, photocopying,
recording or otherwise without the prior permission of the
Copyright owner.

Dales Large Print is an imprint of Library Magna Books Ltd.

Printed and bound in Great Britain by
T.J. (International) Ltd., Cornwall, PL28 8RW

ONE

Jim Burke was sitting on his veranda in his wheelchair when he heard the familiar drumbeats of many horses galloping fast down the trail leading to his ranch holdings.

He'd been drowsy through the heat of the day. Now he perked up and wriggled to a better sitting position. Goddamn his legs! Like lumps of dead meat they were, all because he'd tried to ride a wild stallion and the stallion had won and Jim had been left a mashed-up mess. He'd never ever come to terms with his disability and it had turned him into an irascible old man.

'Goddammit!' he roared in a deep baritone. 'Doesn't someone hear those damned horses? Tom … Jake … where the hell are you? Open the goddamn corral gates or the bastards will be past them and over the hill and Ricky will go crazy!'

At his shout two men emerged from the barn at a run. Jim reckoned they'd been having a spot of shut-eye on the hay, the lazy sons of bitches. They'd been carousing nearly all night and he suspected they were still hung over.

But now he watched them scuttle to the wide double gates, unhooking them and opening them wide enough to make a kind of funnel. The leader of the herd galloped blindly on and the rest followed. As Jim reckoned, they were a mighty fine bunch of horses that Ricky and his boys had rounded up.

Later he got the houseboy to trundle him close to the corral fence so that he could study the milling horses. They were of all colours and sizes. Some would have to be returned to the wild, but there were several that looked promising.

Ricky Latimer came to him, hot and sweaty, a grin covering his stubbled face. He was a man going on forty, slightly bowlegged, an easy mover and as tough as they come.

'What you think of 'em, boss? Found them in one of them there draws, getting fat on that lush grass down by the river. I reckon the leader knew how to look after his herd. He's the best looking horse I've seen in a long time and he's got balls!'

'You think he's good enough for the rodeo?'

'By God, yes! He gave us the runaround before we got them on the go. I tried to bring him down twice, but he's smart, is that one! He outmanoeuvred me!'

'Huh,' grunted Jim Burke, 'then you'll have to get the boys to help you cut him out and get him into the sin bin.'

'Yes, I reckon if we do that and pick out several of his mares and corral them near-by, he'll be rare and mad by next week and I'll bet all next year's pay, nobody will ride him!'

Jim Burke's eyes gleamed. He was a gambling man, it was one of the few pleasures he had left.

'You reckon?'

'Sure. I'm going to bet all the dough I can lay my hands on and take those boys at the Lazy S to the cleaners! It's time we had some luck! Last year they nearly cleaned me out!'

Jim Burke nodded. He too had suffered, for their entrant for the rodeo competition had let them down badly.

'Father!' Both men's heads turned towards the house as Jim Burke's daughter came running out to them. She gave Ricky Latimer a look of dislike before turning her attention to Jim.

'You shouldn't be out in this sun without your hat! You should know better! The last time you did this you finished with a migraine!'

'Stop fussing, girl! I'm merely wanting to see the stallion that's going to win this year's rodeo.'

Milly Burke's lips pursed and turned down at the corners. She didn't approve of Jim's gambling.

'You'd be better off looking over the

accounts! The new scaffolding and the stands are costing way over what was estimated.'

'Look, I'm not interested in all that. We can afford it. We've always put on a fourth of July rodeo and we've always done well, so what's different this year?'

Ricky Latimer looked from one to the other silently. Both had forgotten he was there, so he quietly moved away, back to the corral to supervise the cutting out of the great black stallion and get him fighting mad into a small enclosure of his own.

He was well aware of the tension between father and daughter. They were two of a kind, both strong-willed and stubborn. Since Jim's accident Milly had got quite uppity, as if she was boss of the whole outfit. Ricky didn't envy the man who tried to put a halter around her neck. He'd have an almighty fight! Interesting, no doubt, but life with her would never be a bed of roses.

She was no kid. In some circles she would be classed as an old maid. There had been talk of her being affianced to some young buck who up and went and volunteered when the war broke out, and had been killed at the battle of Cedar Mountain in Virginia, early on in the war. That had been nearly ten years ago and he figured she must be coming up to twenty-eight and turning as mean as any man.

He strode back to the corral and to the business in hand. Those two would just have to scrap it out.

'Pete!' he roared, 'let's get this son of a bitch cut out before the bastard breaks down the fences!'

Milly looked at her father. He was red with rage and frustration. Her heart ached for him. He was so different from the laughing jolly man he used to be. The accident had brought out all the frustration and anger in him. He was a stranger these days.

'Father ... please–'

'Don't you speak to me like that in front of the hands ever again! Do you hear me? I'm not a child to be told what I can do or what I should wear! If I want to risk a migraine, I'll risk one and it's my affair, not yours! Right?'

Milly was bursting with anger inside. It was all very well her father acting up this way, but it was she who had to nurse him when things got rough.

Without a word she turned and stalked back into the house and he could hear pots and pans being thrown about.

He gave a shamefaced grin, then it faded. She was right, but he would never admit that he needed looking after. He shook his head a little. She was a chip off the old block all right!

Inside, in the big kitchen, Milly glared at the old black woman standing at the table kneading dough and up to her elbows in flour.

'Well? Go on, say it! I can tell by your eyes you're wanting to open your mouth to criticize me!'

'Aw, shucks, Miss Milly. If you would only think before you rush in! You know the boss hates any fuss! You're rubbing his nose in the fact that he's only half a man!'

13

Milly sighed.

'I can never do right for him. Sometimes I think I'll marry the first man who asks me, and get away from here!'

Old Annie gave a deep raucous laugh.

'Oh, come on, Miss Milly, things ain't that bad! At least your pa's made good! He's not grubbing about in a two-bit outfit living from hand to mouth! You're a well-respected woman in the community. Everyone looks up to you!'

'And I'm sick of that too! I can't even spit without someone talking about it, and those old crows down at the church look twice if I smile at a man in church!'

Annie laughed again.

'They're only jealous because you've got your freedom. You don't have no man to tell you what you can do or not do!'

'Did you know there was a rumour once that I was a fella hiding under petticoats?'

'Yeah, I heard it. Someone had the cheek to ask me if I noticed anything different about you when you were a baby! I gave them what for, I can tell you!'

Milly stared at her in surprise. 'Why didn't you ever tell me?'

'Because I didn't want to upset you. You've plenty of worries on your shoulders running this place for your pa, without being worried about such a ridiculous thing as that.'

Suddenly Milly grinned. She saw the funny side of the stupid rumour. She had half a mind to run through the yard in just her shift and bloomers during the rodeo. That would shock the churchgoing old biddies. On the other hand, the cowhands would take it as an invitation to become too familiar. She couldn't win.

'Well, I suppose it's no use yacking. How's the grub coming along?'

'I'm on with the last batch of bread. The pickled beef's ready to come out of the barrel, and the cookies are ready. I've got all the makin's ready for the pancakes. I'll be up bright and early to make them on the morning. Old Ikey's out back chopping wood for the barbecue and he's got the sides of beef ready to put on the spits.'

'Good. What about the beer?'

'All brewed up ready in the barrels and the boss said to bring up a couple of cases of his best whiskey for the ranchers.'

'You seem to have everything in hand.'

'Yeah, no sweat. Just the same as last year and the year before that.' The old woman's white teeth flashed in her round face.

Milly put an arm about her shoulders and hugged her.

'I don't know what I'd do without you, Annie. You're a gem!'

'Just remember that when you finally marry! I want to be the one who catches your posy of flowers!'

Milly laughed and went to the kitchen door. She looked back.

'Some hopes, Annie. I'm a confirmed spinster. I don't want no man telling me what to do!'

Annie shook her head as she went on kneading dough. That was the trouble with that girl. She had no notion of what

16

running in double harness could be. It wasn't all about having your own way. It was caring for someone. Old Annie's eyes misted over as she thought of that man of hers all those years ago and how good it had been. Too good. He'd been shot by his owner and she'd been left broken-hearted. It was then she'd escaped from her birth-place and drifted, hungry and frightened, until she had been taken on by Jim Burke and his wife, who were expecting a baby. She'd stayed ever since, looking after Milly when Mrs Burke died of a fever. There had been no man in her life after her man was killed.

Milly went to change her skirt and blouse for shirt and riding-pants. She wanted to help with the choosing and cutting out of the new intake of mustangs.

She was proud of her knowledge of good and bad animals. Her father had always treated her as the son he never had and she knew what made a good riding-horse or a good cow horse with the best.

Horses came in many guises. Some were leaders and others were content to follow. A really good cow pony, which could cut out and run a wild mustang, was worth much more than a horse only fit to be a pack-animal. There were horses which reacted naturally to the sounds of a horn. They were natural chargers, having the courage to gallop into battle, and were not fazed by cannon fire or shrieks and shouts.

Jim Burke had built up a good reputation for breaking in good horses for the army and for the caravan trade. A would-be buyer could come and describe what he wanted and Jim had always been proud of the fact he could come up with the ideal horse.

Milly expected to be able to carry on that tradition.

She joined Ricky Latimer at the rails as he watched a couple of the bronc-busters chasing and lassooing the mustangs. The big black stallion was still screaming defiance as the mares and foals were being cut out of the herd.

Milly climbed the rails and sat beside Ricky.

'You think we'll have a chance with that stallion?'

'By God, if we haven't then we'll give up! I don't think the Lazy S boys will come up with anything so good!'

Milly looked at Ricky with amusement. He was like her father in never referring to the Goodison brothers by name, both referred to them as 'those Lazy S boys'.

The fact was, they weren't boys any longer. Three brothers, the eldest now going on fifty by Milly's calculations, and the youngest nearly thirty. She reckoned her father wouldn't even remember their forenames … Luke, Jonas and the young 'un known as Buster.

Years ago when the Goodisons and the Burkes had first settled on the land, there had been disputes over fences and water rights; those disputes flared up even now, periodically.

Jim Burke considered the Lazy S boys to

be nothing more than reformed rustlers now that their old man was dead.

He viewed their stray cattle and horses on his land with suspicion and was always exhorting Milly and the hands to watch out for rustling and brand-changing.

Milly reckoned it was an obsession with her father, the result of his accident and having the time to brood.

There was not much communication between the two ranches during the year, but at the Fourth of July celebrations the Goodisons came with the rest of the ranchers and brought their best unbroken horse to the competition.

Last year they had been unpopular winners of the contest. Even the other ranchers fought shy of much contact with the Goodison boys and their crew, for they tended to be rowdy and quarrelsome when they'd drunk too much and several heated quarrels had broken out amongst the visiting crews.

This year Milly was determined that the disgraceful scenes would not be repeated.

The beer for the men would be restricted and the hard liquor for the ranchers, rationed. They could call her a spoilsport if they liked. She couldn't care a toss what they thought.

The next four days were busy with organizing and putting up the stands and temporary showground. Bunting was brought out and hung and several tattered flags flew above the living-quarters of the men, and the main house. It all looked very gay.

The barbecues were built, huge long lines of firewood, ready to start burning to make a thick mass of charcoal ready for the spits. The sides of beef would take a full day to cook slowly, and several small boys were put in charge of turning the spits at intervals.

There was ginger beer to make for the ladies, and several new privies had to be dug in discreet places amongst the trees for both males and females. Nothing had been forgotten.

The visitors began arriving just after dawn. Ladies from the nearby ranches came in buggies bringing their offerings of pies

Roscommon County Library Service
WITHDRAWN
FROM STOCK

21

and cakes and their own speciality, like pressed beef and tongue and pork patties.

Trestle-tables were already waiting for the offerings and were soon filled. Two young girls were bribed with soda pops to wave fans over the food and drive away the flies.

Then came the wagons containing the horses, surrounded by a number of cowboys. The closed wagons reverberated to the kicks and squeals of maddened animals. They were the lucky ones.

The poorer ranchers brought their entrants on foot, four men hanging on to ropes while the frightened animal frothed and kicked every step of the way. The owners reckoned that that was the way to get a beast good and mad; when the time came for him to be ridden, he'd kick the hell out of any rider who dared to bestride him.

The local doctor was on hand. He was the busiest man at any rodeo, and reckoned to earn himself more dough in one day than he did in six months!

At last, mid-morning, on the stroke of ten,

the big iron triangle was beaten, the rodeo was beginning and lots were drawn as to which horses went first and who would ride them.

The crowds were already set, the cowboy crews at the rails to cheer their man on, and the older people, the ladies and children stood on their wagons to get a good view. The wagons ringed the whole showground.

Milly reckoned it was a good turnout and was pleased for her father.

She could hear the odds being shouted as the mayor of their nearest town, Sweetwater, took charge of this most important chore. He was the man everyone trusted not to make off with the cash. He was known as an honest man.

It was a knockout contest. Men thrown were eliminated. Horses broken in were also eliminated. During the morning, seven horses were eliminated and a dozen men. The afternoon would see the contest come to a climax.

It would be the most fiery horse which

had not been broken, and the man who had not been unseated who would come together for the final showdown. Bets would be high on both man and beast.

All were agog to watch the outcome.

Noon came and went before the first preliminaries were over.

Milly's eye had been caught by a stranger, a huge man who stood out in the crowd of big men. He was unkempt and dirty, as if he'd ridden far and not stopped to wash or even sluice his head in a horse trough.

He'd watched the contestants from a distance; when the first flush of riders had been unhorsed he'd casually elbowed his way to the front rail, climbed over and spoken to one of the judges near him. The judge, old Amos Childs, had nodded and given the dusty newcomer the go-ahead.

'Ladies and gentlemen,' bawled Amos, 'we have a new contestant. His name is Judd!'

A hush went over the crowd. This was interesting, for there were no bets on his past performances. Everyone was waiting to jeer him when he was thrown by the fiery roan.

At first Judd stalked the stallion, lariat in hand. The beast got a whiff of his smell, and his head came up, his eyes gleamed wickedly and he screamed defiance, then kicked up his hindquarters, legs lashing out viciously.

Everyone held their breath. This stallion was a ball-breaker.

Suddenly, Judd had spun the lariat during one of the stallion's wildest lunges and brought his head down hard. The stallion rolled on to his side, all four legs kicking. Judd hung on until the animal quietened, then allowed him to struggle to his feet.

Judd ran his hand over his head and back while the horse's eyes rolled showing the whites. The crowd could hear him murmur something softly to the animal.

There was an expectant silence in the crowd and Milly, looking about her, realized that all attention was on Judd. There was hardly a breath being drawn.

Then Judd's lariat was being wound around the animal's head like a bridle and he was being pulled forward. That was when the stallion went mad, rearing and trumpeting. That was the moment Judd leapt aboard, knees tightening about the belly. Lariat rope in one hand, his hat in the other, he rode the beast. The crowd cheered and shrieked while man and horse stomped and reached for the sky.

The stallion arched his back and came down stiff-legged. The jolting of the man's body was felt by every cowpoke watching. Then the stallion tried other tactics: rearing and kicking, galloping and stopping with sudden jerks. And yet Judd clung on. There was blood pouring from his nose from a blow from a rearing head. It ran down the front of his dirty shirt and on to the horse's mane. But Judd hung on.

Suddenly it was all over. The roan was exhausted. It quivered a little, took several slow steps and stood, head hung low.

Then the crowd watched as Judd spoke softly to it, hands caressing and patting. Suddenly the animal lifted his head and nickered softly and both man and horse trotted slowly around the arena.

The crowd went wild.

Later, Milly watched the stranger take on another animal that had bested all comers. Again the tussle between man and beast. Again, the man's will was stronger than his opponent's.

Now Milly was watching Judd with interest. Where was he from? Where was he heading? They could do with a man like him, a super bronc-buster. She wondered if he would offer to ride their stallion.

She glanced at her father. Was he too thinking he would be a good man to hire?

'Father,' she said softly, 'are you thinking what I'm thinking?'

He looked at her, his eyes grim.

'I don't reckon so. What are you thinking?'

'That this stranger, Judd, might be useful to us. We could offer to hire him…'

'I don't think so. He's dangerous. I don't want him on my property! If he comes, set the dogs on him!'

'Father!'

'You heard me? That's an order!'

'But why?'

'We locked horns years ago. I recognized him as soon as he walked into the arena. He's bad medicine, Milly. So keep well away from him!'

TWO

For a moment there was silence between the two. Then Milly plucked up her courage to say softly,

'It was something to do with that range war.' It was a statement, not a question.

For a long moment she thought he wasn't going to answer her, then he sighed.

'Yes, but I don't want to talk about it!'

'I remember you left Ma and me. I was only a nipper. We cried, for Ma was left to look after the stock and I had to carry buckets of swill for the pigs. It was then she lost the baby–'

'For God's sake! That happened twenty years ago!' He wriggled helplessly in his chair. 'We should both forget all that!'

'She died because you were away from us! How can you want to forget all that?' she shouted, suddenly bitter and angry.

'Look, Milly, I know I shouldn't have left you both, but I considered defending my land more important than anything else in the world! I'd worked hard to own and run this land, and I didn't want a bastard like Isaac Judd taking over that dog-leg piece we own further down the valley. It was *my* land and I was going to see that it remained mine!'

'And that was when you locked horns with that man's father?'

'Yes, dammit! I caught him red-handed. Him and his son were fencing off my land and I wasn't going to argue about it. I shot him and that teenage son beat me up and when I was down and helpless on my back, he deliberately shot me in the shoulder and said, "That's to remember me by!" Then the kid puked all over me! I passed out and when I came round, he and his father were gone. I was lucky to be alive.'

'I remember you coming home covered with blood and I was so scared I went to hide in the hay loft!'

'So now you know why he's here. Keep away from him, Milly, d'you hear?'

'But why, after all these years?'

'God knows, but he'll have something in mind.'

The afternoon wore on and at last there were two horses left and three victorious cowboys. Judd was one of them.

The crowd, now fed and liquored up, waited in anticipation for some real horsemanship. Bets were struck and Milly saw her father perk up a little as he was surrounded more and more by would-be gamblers. Gambling gave him the buzz necessary to enliven a frustrating life.

The other animal in contention was owned by the Goodison brothers, a huge seventeen-hands-high beast with rolling eyes and flashing teeth. Already his chestnut coat was flecked with foam and Milly reckoned half his strength had been dissipated through nervous jitters. The men cast lots who should ride first.

Milly watched as the Goodison horse was hauled, prancing and screaming into the ring by four of the Goodison crew. All were sweating and it took some considerable time to let him loose. When he was finally freed of his ropes he moved like a bullet round and round the arena.

Then a rancher's son leapt into the ring, lariat in hand, and the battle was on to the cheering of the drunken crowd.

The moment came when the youth finally snared the animal's head and leapt on to his back. He lasted a minute by the judge's watch, then he reached for the sky, coming down with a sickening bump. A great sigh went up from the crowd, then came silence as two men leapt over the rails and carried the inert figure away. Someone yelled for the doctor who was quietly imbibing whiskey from a barrel set up beside the trestle-tables.

Judd was the last to ride. He watched impassively as the second man took on the Goodison horse. This time the battle lasted longer but again the cowboy was unseated. He rolled away as the horse's front legs came down to kick daylight into him.

Judd watched the horse gallop frenziedly around the ring. Suddenly he threw away his lariat and waited … and waited. The crowd grew impatient and catcalls split the hot dry air.

'Get on with it!'

'Lost your balls?'

'Either shape up or give up!'

But Judd ignored the taunts and waited. Then the beast slowed his gait. It was as if curiosity was overcoming his temper. He trotted and the circle grew smaller until at last Judd reckoned it was the right time to strike. With one giant leap he swung himself aboard and clung tightly to the stallion's mane before groping for the bridle.

Then the fun began. The beast, affronted by the sudden attack and the weight on his back, leapt and reared, sprang upwards as if on iron springs, coming down hard, his back bowed, jarring every bone in Judd's body. The animal screamed defiance, trying to unseat the unwanted creature on his back.

The crowd howled in pleasure. Every man there could appreciate every bone-jarring jolt, admire the hard vicelike grip of the legs and the sheer damned determination to hang on there even if the world went upside down.

At last the horse shivered and stood with head down. Judd spoke softly and stroked the long neck. Quietly the animal took several quivering steps and then stood still.

Judd slid from the saddle and handed the reins to one of the judges.

'Take him away and rub him down. I think he's got rid of his devils!'

The crowd waited. Would he now take on their host's horse? It was customary for the winner of the preliminary contests to have a choice. He could take on Jim Burke's entrant or decline after a battle such as Judd had gone through and no man would blame him. It would take a strong man to stand up to a second such contest.

The judges conferred and Judd consulted and then the announcement came.

'Ladies and gentlemen, the winner here, Judd, will ride Mr Burke's horse but there will be a half-hour's interval. Those who need to refresh themselves can now do so!'

A great cheer went up. More free beer and still more entertainment. If Judd broke in Burke's horse he would get an additional $1000 on top of the prize he had already won.

There was much speculation and the betting was increased. Those watching the Goodison brothers saw how disgruntled they were at the outcome of the last challenge.

Those in the know reckoned there would be bloodshed before the day was over. The doc had better watch his drinking.

Judd stalked off on his own and sluiced his

shaggy head in the horse trough. Milly watched him from a distance. He moved stiffly. Milly reckoned every bone in his body must ache. He might be a dangerous guy but he was a courageous one.

She held her breath when eventually the great black stallion, accompanied by four of Jim Burke's men, was finally brought into the ring. The ropes came off him and the men sprang away, all leaping for the rails.

Judd was there but this time he kept hold of his lariat. He waited as the animal screamed defiance and reared up in front of him, his forefeet weaving like a boxer's feet. A glancing blow could have smashed Judd's head in.

Then the lariat snaked over the head, the loop closing and coming down hard. The animal dropped to the ground and Judd swiftly wrapped his lariat around the kicking front legs. Then, as the animal struggled to rise, he waited. As it came up on four legs, Judd vaulted into the saddle.

The crowd were disappointed. This was

not going to be a full-blooded battle. Man's cunning was winning over brute strength.

Then came the stomping as the beast panicked, trying to free his front legs. He sky-dived, and hump-backed but the weight on him did not shift.

At last, all defiance was dissipated and the animal's head hung low. The crowd watched the quivering legs and the shivering body.

The crowd were disgusted. They'd been robbed of a spectacular and Jim Burke was furious. The best, most fiery horse he'd had in years, and he'd turned out like some corny four-year-old! He couldn't believe it! And the bastard who'd turned a winner into a has-been was the son of the man he had shot!

He turned to Milly.

'You do the honours! Give him the prize money and tell him to get out … fast!'

'But, Father–'

'I said tell him to get out! I don't want him on the place!'

'But the winner usually stays the night for the party!'

'I don't care a damn! I just want him off my place. Now will you tell him or shall I get Ricky to throw him out?'

Milly's mouth set firmly.

'I'll tell him. Ricky will only start a fight.'

'Then do it!' Jim Burke motioned to a couple of houseboys. He was lifted off the wagon in his chair and was trundled indoors.

Milly joined the judges in the ring and was given the two prizes. She waited with unusual nervous anticipation to hand them over to the big stranger.

She waited alongside the judges. Where was he? What was keeping him? She nervously bit her fingernails as she waited.

Then he came, leaping over the rails and walking in long purposeful strides towards them. He had cleaned himself up and brushed the dust from his clothes. He looked much more presentable.

She gave a little speech which for the life of her she couldn't remember afterwards, his bright blue eyes disconcerting her. Father had never mentioned his blue eyes!

Then all embarrassment left her when he thanked her in a deep velvety soft voice and explained that he couldn't stay as he was expected elsewhere. Instead, she was nonplussed, having steeled herself for the unpleasant job of asking him to leave the property.

'Oh! You'll miss the party!' she blurted out. His blue eyes twinkled.

'I'm not exactly dressed for a party.' Before she could answer he turned and waved his hands in a victory salute to all those watching, the noise from the crowd drowning anything Milly might have said in reply.

It gave her time to think what a fool she was. Her words about the party! He might so easily have changed his mind. She must be going loco … and all for a pair of blue eyes!

Then with a polite bow to her he jumped down from the wagon and disappeared into the crowd.

The rest of the evening was taken over by the dancers. Two fiddlers and a man with a Jew's harp set the pace with some of the old traditional square-dance tunes. Milly recognized the 'Turkey Trot' and the popular 'She'll be comin' round the mountain when she comes' and her feet began to tap.

Soon couples were dancing on the space in front of the ranch house, while the oldsters and those with two left feet sat around and watched and drank Jim Burke's barrels of beer dry.

There was no lack of partners for Milly, for young unwed women were few and far between. Cowboys danced together in a lumbering gait but all enjoyed the music and the ragged singing.

As Milly danced with one partner after another she noticed that the Goodison brothers were missing. Thinking back, she'd never seen them since Judd's departure. Uneasily, she wondered whether Judd's breaking the Goodison horse had anything to do with their departure. Then she remembered the prize money. Judd would have $1500 on him… But it was no concern of hers. After all, he was a stranger.

She put both the Goodisons and Judd out of her mind and enjoyed the party. She only wished her father would attend these affairs, but he had explained that he couldn't bear to watch the dancers, for it brought back memories of himself and her mother dancing together in their early days before their marriage.

It was the one time in the year when she felt truly feminine. The rest of the time, even at Christmas, she felt like one of the boys and the men treated her as such.

Tonight was a night to remember.

She rested while her latest partner went to find her a glass of Annie's homemade lemonade. She was hot and sweaty, and fanned herself with a broad leaf from their one shade tree, having no fancy fan.

It was then the fight broke out. A shot was fired, and Milly began to run towards the crowd. She fought her way through, elbowing anyone who got in her way, then stood and watched as two men were being dragged apart and a woman was being held up by a couple of cowboys, her dress soaked in blood.

'What's happened?' Milly gasped.

'Lance Broadbent objected to one of Goodison's crew flirting with his woman. There'll be hell to pay!'

'What about the woman?'

'She jumped in front of Lance and took the bullet. If the doc doesn't get here quick she looks as if she'll bleed to death!'

'Oh, God … I'll have to go to her!' Milly rushed forward to help, but she was too late. The woman sagged between the two men and she heard one of them mutter:

'Goddammit! She's gone!' They laid her gently on the ground.

Immediately there were yells of anger from the watching crowd. The once cheery audience had now turned nasty and Milly was conscious of the smell of danger in the air.

'Lynch the bastard!' roared one tough cowboy who'd been a contestant. 'We all saw what happened! That son of a bitch aimed to kill Broadbent! He don't need no jury to judge his intent. I say string him up!'

'Aye, aye...' shouted many voices. 'None of the Lazy S crew is any good! They're all rustlers and killers! String him up!'

There was a rush of men and Lance Broadbent was knocked over as they surged towards the man who'd started the fight by pestering Lance's woman. Now she was dead.

They dragged the kicking cowhand to the shade tree in the ranch yard. Milly watched with horror. They were mad, all of them! Even the women were baying for blood.

'You can't do that!' she screamed. 'It's the Fourth of July! You can't lynch him. He must have a fair trial!'

But her voice was lost in the uproar. Only a few folk close by heard her words and they laughed at her.

Wildly she wondered what to do next. Then she thought of her father's shotgun. She rushed into the house to lift it off its hooks on the wall. She was blazing mad that the ungrateful crowd out there should think of profaning their land with a lynching! If it came to pass, it would be forever etched on her brain and this home of hers would never be the same again.

Outside, she lifted up her skirts and ran, the shotgun pointing to the sky. She was in time to see a rope being flung over a branch, the noose around the man's neck. His head hung low as if already he'd received severe punishment.

She elbowed her way through the packed watchers and then fired the shotgun into the sky. At once there was an expectant stillness amongst the drunken blood-hungry throng. She sent another shot into the air for good measure, and then turned to the men holding the prisoner.

'Hold it, you fellers! I'm not having this man hanged on this land! Take him to Sweetwater and let the sheriff send for the judge and try him properly.'

'What! And have the Lazy S crew come charging in and shooting up the jail to free him? Not on your life!' The man, who seemed to be the spokesman, spat on the ground. 'We hang him now!'

Milly raised the shotgun again, but a large hand stopped her. She looked up and saw the stranger, Judd, at her side.

He looked own at her and smiled.

'You'll have to load up again, lady, but in the meanwhile I think this will stop 'em.' He withdrew a heavy Peacemaker from its holster and waved it unerringly at the men in front of him.

'Do as the little lady says, mister. Tie him up and I'll get him to Sweetwater. I guarantee it!'

It was a stalemate, and Bob Penrose, the man who'd taken charge, looked into the unwavering barrel and saw menace there. There was also a cool calculating look in the stranger's blue eyes. He gave way reluctantly.

'Very well, mister. You be responsible for him but some of us will ride with you. How do we know you're not in with the Goodisons?'

Judd gave a wicked smile.

'You don't, but I tell you this, I wouldn't want to lie dead beside any of them!'

Milly looked up at him. She had just got over the sensation he'd roused when he'd called her a little lady. He made her feel all woman. Now she wondered at his tone. It sounded as if he knew the Goodisons. Maybe he wasn't in this neighbourhood because of her father. Maybe it was the Goodisons he was after...

The rope came down off the tree and the prisoner's hands were tied together.

Milly turned to Judd.

'Thank you for your help,' she said softly. Then she took her courage in both hands and said a little defiantly. 'My father recognized you. He thought you were after him!'

Judd nodded.

'He killed my father in a dispute over land. I was there. I had the chance to kill him but I hadn't the guts. I was only a kid of seventeen, so I shot him in the shoulder. Did he tell you this?'

'Yes, and I remember him coming home covered in blood. I was only eight at the time and very scared. Why are you leaving him alone now?'

'Because I reckon killing him would be a merciful release for him. He suffers more sitting in that chair of his than I could inflict with a bullet! I think he's got all he deserves!' He turned away from her and joined the men holding the prisoner.

Anger flooded her, dissipating any friendly feelings she might have had for him. The son of a bitch was no better than any of the uncouth cowhands she encountered and she despised the lot of them!

She went off to find Annie, who no doubt needed all the help she could get. Annie reckoned that the visiting women only got in the way, that they didn't come to do any real work, just to get together and have a gossip.

Matthew Judd looked after her. She was a mighty fine filly with enough temper to make the taming of her interesting. He had a mind to have a go when he'd finished his business with the Goodisons.

His attention was taken to the prisoner, who eyed him from under bushy eyebrows.

'I be in your debt, stranger,' the prisoner said gruffly. 'What will it take to let me go free? The boss will pay!'

Judd laughed and yanked the ropes binding both wrists to see they were secure.

'Sorry to disappoint you, mister, but I take very badly to being bribed! You aimed to kill the man but you got the woman. In my eyes you should hang, but I believe in doing the job properly with the judge and all. I'll get you to Sweetwater, never fear!'

The man's teeth showed in a snarl as he growled:

'You'll be lucky! When Luke hears what's happened, he'll be rare and mad! He and the boys will come after us and then you'll be wolf bait! I'm warning you, fella, you let me go and you'll save yourself a mess of trouble!'

'Why should he go to all that trouble over you?'

'Because I'm one of his best *pistoleros,*

that's why!'

'So would you like to show me what you can do?'

There was a gasp from the crowd standing by. What kind of a fool was this stranger called Judd? He could tame an unbroken horse, had legs like steel bands, but what kind of a guy was he with a gun? This all sounded sensational. Were they going to see a battle between two professional gunmen? Or were they going to see a braggart end up hitting dirt and the prisoner going free?

The crowd were pushing closer to listen to every word.

'Well?' taunted Judd, 'are you all mouth and hot air?' and he stood easily with legs apart, shoulders thrown back, as relaxed as any man could be in this situation. 'Or maybe you've just got a yeller streak where your backbone should be!'

The man growled and shook his wrists at him.

'Untie me, and I'll show you what I can do!' Then he looked around the crowd.

'Now hear me, and hear me good! When I kill him, I go free and I'll kill any man who trys to stop me!' The watching men were silent … waiting.

The old man in charge of the wild-horse contest stepped forward and, with two cuts, severed the ropes binding the man's wrists. He stepped back sharply out of harm's way.

The man glared at Judd as he rubbed his wrists and flexed his fingers.

Judd stood his ground and the crowd suddenly realized that the challenge was being taken up. Everyone looked at Judd and as the men scattered there were suddenly a flurry of hasty bets on the outcome.

The old judge stepped forward again.

'If you want a referee…' Judd waved him away, his eyes never leaving the prisoner's hands.

'Get out of the way, mister. This is between me and him.' He watched as the man took several steps backwards.

Judd's eyes narrowed as he watched the man's body language. There was the slight stiffening of the back, the legs unbent a little, the arms, stiff at the man's side, moved just the slightest, then the body suddenly leapt to life and fell into the gunman's crouch.

The men watching said they never saw Judd's hand move to his holster in one smooth practised action before the prisoner's gun was out of its holster. Two shots, and the crimson stained the man's shirt as the impact of the slugs punched him backwards before he slumped to the ground.

For a long moment there was silence as they watched Judd holster his gun and turn away. They watched him with respect.

Turning to the old man who'd offered to referee, he said brusquely:

'Send him back to the Goodisons with my compliments. Tell them the name's Judd. They'll understand!'

Then he strode off to find his horse. They watched him ride away as they heaved the corpse on to his own horse and someone reluctantly offered to take the corpse and the message to the Goodison ranch.

THREE

Luke Goodison watched the unbroken stallion plunge and rear as it was released into the corral. He'd been bitterly disappointed that the big man had bested the son of a bitch. He was half-inclined to set him free to find his herd. He would probably be more useful siring good foals. He was the kind of beast that needed his spirit to be broken to make a good saddle horse, and everyone knew that a spiritless horse never made the grade.

His thoughts were interrupted by a shout from his foreman.

'Hey, boss, there's a couple of riders coming down the trail!'

Luke turned his mare so that he could take a look. He screwed his eyes up against the evening sun's glare. It must be Jody coming

51

in with a stranger. He and his brothers had left the rodeo early in disgust. They hadn't wanted to witness Jim Burke crowing over them.

The crew had drifted back in small bunches. None of the men was popular with the surrounding ranchers and the small-time dirt farmers. They'd drunk their fill of Jim Burke's liquor and high-tailed it before trouble started. All were back but Jody.

He look a long hard look. That wasn't Jody riding his mare. He didn't recognize the guy, and what in hell was on the back of the horse he was leading?

Then he recognized Jody's mustang. It had clear brown-and-white markings. It couldn't possibly be Jody dumped in the saddle like a sack of flour? He was a professional gunman, goddammit! He waited with a cold feeling in his guts.

But it was Jody, slung over the nervous animal, who smelled death on his back. The man leading the animal looked warily at Luke Goodison.

'I was told to bring you your *pistolero*. The guy who sent him with his compliments is called Judd. He said you would understand!'

Luke Goodison drew in a deep breath. Judd! There had been something about the feller that made him uneasy when he'd first seen him. Something in the walk or the way he'd thrown his shoulders back, but the beard and unkempt hair had fooled him. Judd! So the bastard was out of jail, and by the look of things was gunning for him and Jonas!

It had been more than twenty years since he and Jonas had bribed Judge Gannon in Nashville, Tennessee, to bring in a guilty verdict with evidence they had concocted about a bank robbery they and their men had set up. Matthew Judd had been in the bank at the wrong time. He'd been knocked out by Luke and a wad of stolen notes stuffed down his trousers, and Matthew, only twenty-two and inexperienced, hadn't had a chance.

He was sent to the pen for twenty years,

and Luke Goodison had congratulated himself on quick thinking and a judge who could be bribed. Now he calculated that Judd must have just come out of jail.

He smelled trouble. He swore at the man who'd brought Jody back to the ranch.

'You can go back to the bastard and tell him I'll be waiting for him.'

'I cain't do that, boss. He moseyed out of town just after the shooting!'

'Hell! He could be anywhere on the range!' He turned and whistled for his foreman.

'Greg, find Jonas, pronto! I've got news for him!' Then he turned to the man. 'Well? What are you waiting for? Get to hell out of it!'

'It's been a hard slog bringing that corpse here. That horse of his had the jitters. It was thirsty work!'

Luke dug into his vest pocket and produced a silver dollar.

'Here, catch. Have a drink on me!'

The man's eyes lit up.

'Thanks, boss. I'll drink to your good

health!' He grinned. 'You'll need all the luck you can get. That Judd feller is sure some humdinger of a shootist! I don't envy any man he goes after!' With that he dug his heels into his horse's ribs and rode away.

Jonas, along with the youngest brother, Buster, rode up, both watching the rider loping along the trail.

'What's up, Luke? Why the all-fired hurry? We was just in the middle of settling down the mares and foals for the night.'

'That can wait,' Luke said grimly. He pointed to the horse and its burden now being led away towards the barn.

'Who's the stiff, and who put daylight through him?'

'You remember that kid, Judd?'

'You mean the kid we railroaded into taking the rap for that botched-up bank robbery?'

'Not so loud, you fool! Yes, that's the one. Well, he's out there somewhere and he's gunning for us!'

Jonas looked shocked while young Buster looked from one to the other of his brothers.

He wasn't used to seeing them in a panic.

'What's this all about, Luke?' Buster asked sharply. 'What's this about a robbery?'

Luke turned savagely at him.

'Keep out of this, Buster! It's none of your business!'

'But if there's something wrong, I should know!'

Luke's reaction was quick. He wasn't used to being questioned by anyone, least of all his still wet-behind-the-ears brother. He leaned forward and smacked Buster's horse smartly on the rump. The horse leapt in the air and galloped away.

Luke stared pensively after him.

'We're going to have trouble with that boy!' Jonas looked uneasy.

'Luke, maybe we should put him straight. If Judd is gunning for us, then the whole mess is going to come out. We can't keep the kid in ignorance for ever!'

Luke, a thick set man running to fat, grizzled, his coarse face showing years of hard drinking and womanising, turned red.

Jonas often thought that one day Luke would fall down in a fit during one of his mad rages.

'Now, take it easy, Luke. It was just a notion...'

'Then keep your notions to yourself! You weren't exactly born with the sharpest brain! If it wasn't for me, you'd be jail bait now!'

'Aw, that's not fair, Luke! I pull my weight!'

'Yes, under orders!'

Jonas flushed. He hated being spoken to like some kid, and he a man going on forty. Sometimes he thought Luke regarded him and Buster as two useless hangers-on. But of course it had been Luke's brains that had gotten them this ranch in the first place. If it hadn't been for Luke they would all have been just itinerant cowboys going from one ranch to another. Life had been hard after the war; both of them had come home to find their parents dead and young Buster being cared for by neighbours.

Jonas would never forget that disastrous

bank robbery, when things had gone wrong, and the hard cash they'd managed to prise from the bank's vaults had been handed over to the local judge, George Gannon. They'd escaped jail by the skin of their teeth. All that had been kept from the kid, not because the knowledge might upset him but because Luke didn't trust him not to spill the beans at some time. Jonas had to give Luke some credit. There'd been other raids and in the end, after a bit of rustling on the side and some shady deals, they'd got what Luke had aimed for, a nice parcel of land. As the years had gone on they'd squeezed out several small ranchers until the Lazy S was one of the biggest spreads in Kentucky.

He also knew that Luke's ambitions weren't all over. He wanted Jim Burke's land and Jonas was sure that some day Luke would damn well succeed. It was only a matter of time. Luke wouldn't let a cripple stand in his way to total power.

Of course there was that stuck up spirited filly to consider but Luke could soon run rings round a slip of a girl. Luke had once mentioned kidnap, but he'd been drinking. Luke had laughed and said that Buster could violate her and then they would have to marry and they'd get the ranch that way. But that had been in Luke's cups.

Now he looked at his brother.

'Then what do we do about Judd?'

'We'll go out there, you and me, and we'll kill him!'

Matthew Judd looked at the sky, calculating how long it would take him to reach Sweetwater. He patted his mare's neck and then dug his heels gently into her ribs, a sign for her to lengthen her stride to a canter she could keep up for hours.

Both man and horse enjoyed the swift movement, the quiet, and the animal knew she was heading for a warm stable, some oats and sweet-smelling hay.

Judd patted his vest pocket, feeling the comforting wad of notes. It had been a long time since he'd seen that amount of hard cash. He grinned. He was going to have a high old time visiting the barber and if he was lucky he could take a hot bath with real soap. A rare luxury!

It had been so long since he'd seen his unshaven face, he probably wouldn't recognize himself. Thoughts of bathing reminded him of his ragged and torn clothes. He knew he must smell bad. He wondered what that spirited daughter of Jim Burke thought of him. He comforted himself that she must be used to evil-smelling men around her. At least now he could get a whole new rig-out, from vest and underpants upwards. He had the cash to pay.

There was another reason why he should change his image. It had taken two years to find Judge Gannon and Luke Goodison and he wanted every advantage.

A year had been lopped off his sentence because he'd saved the life of the governor of the penitentiary. A crazed convict had broken free of the chain-gang party that they'd both been part of and when the governor had come to inspect them and turned his back on Cass Turner, Judd had seen the murder glint in Turner's eyes. Fortunately Judd had been next to Turner and yelled a warning as the governor turned his back on them both. Judd had felled the man to the ground and wrested a metal stake from the man's hand. A grateful governor had order his release, much to Judd's surprise.

He'd spent that year and the next in trailing the judge and the Goodisons from Tennessee to Kentucky. Now he'd found them. First, he would tackle the Goodisons. That way they would not be alerted by the judge. Gannon could wait. He was now an old man going on seventy.

He knew he'd made a mistake in entering the contest at the Burke ranch, but he couldn't resist taking a look at his father's murderer. He'd been shocked by the old man in the wheelchair, but also impressed by his daughter. Also the thought of a ready-cash prize had finally persuaded him to take part.

He wondered if the Goodison brothers

had recognized him. Now at least, they would know he was in the area. He'd been a fool to send that message, but there, he'd always been a fool or else he would never have finished up in the pen.

The sun was sinking fast when he entered the narrow defile that cut through giant boulders. It would take at least an hour to ride through it. He could take it easy. Maybe stay overnight, and find some shelter. Both he and the mare could do with some rest. He could tackle Sweetwater in the morning.

His eyes wandered from force of habit over the rugged landscape, seeking a good place to camp for the night. He spied a trickle of water obviously coming from a spring further up the defile. He soon found it by the sparse greenery growing around it. An ideal place to spend the night.

Making a small fire, he brewed coffee from the makings he carried in his saddle-bags. There were the remains of a stale hunk of bread and several slices of pickled pork. The meagre fare was very much in contrast to the lavish spread at the Burke rodeo, but it would suffice. He lay down to sleep by the dying fire, the mare tethered close by. She was as good as a guard if strangers or wild animals approached the camp.

He was up and drinking coffee well before dawn. Soon he was packed up and ready to ride. He was keen to reach Sweetwater and looked forward to his shave and bath. Now he thought about it, he was itchy and he combed his hair and beard with his fingers to see if there were lice lurking in the matted curls.

They were nearly at the end of the narrow pass when the shot came. It pinged off the rocky wall a few feet in front of the mare. Her reaction was to squeal and rear and Judd crouched low, cursing as he urged the beast on to a faster gallop.

Two more shots came. Whoever was shooting was no mean gunman but the mare was now galloping at a headlong pace. Then Judd saw the two rearing rocks standing like giant teeth and immediately wheeled his mount to one side. He leapt off, reached for his rifle and crouched low, watching the backover trail while the mare stamped and heaved and drew breath.

Judd's eyes narrowed as he saw the two riders. They were coming at full tilt around a curve in the narrow trail. He was sure the leader was Luke Goodison himself, from what he could remember of the man from twenty-one years ago. The man must be pushing fifty by this time. The other man could be his brother...

Judd's lips parted in a wolfish smile. This was payback time. He would get one chance to shoot before they took cover. Luke Goodison would be the target, the younger brother could be taken care of at a later date.

Patiently he waited. This was the moment he'd waited for for so many years, the anticipation had sustained him, kept him alive when lesser men would have died. He screwed his eyes from the early morning sun, then as the two men galloped towards him, he let off two shots. The first slammed into

Luke Goodison's shoulder and the next hit the man's horse in the neck. He watched as Luke Goodison half-rose into the air, then the horse reared and hit the ground fast, tossing Goodison into a rib-crushing heap on to the ground. Judd saw with satisfaction that the man did not move again. His companion leapt from his moving horse, hit the track and rolled away behind the stump of a long-dead tree.

Then came a flurry of shots but it was obvious that the man, if he were Jonas Goodison, had not registered where the assault was coming from. Judd grinned. He remembered at the trial how slow-witted Jonas Goodison had been and how far he'd been under his older brother's thumb.

He reckoned his fight was with Luke, not Jonas. If Luke was dead, then he could go on and seek out Judge Gannon and wreak his vengeance on him.

Suddenly the obsession that had governed his life for so long seemed trivial. It was nearly over, and it dawned on him that now he must make a new life and start again.

His thoughts turned to Milly Burke. Goddammit! He was only thirty-seven if his mother had told the truth about the date of his birth. He could put all the past years behind him, find a place to call home, marry and bring up a family. The idea intrigued him. He'd never known any respectable women. Those he'd encountered had either been saloon girls or tarts from the city brothels, and up until now he'd not had a lot of respect for females.

But Milly Burke was different. It would take a real man to bring her to heel. He laughed. What in hell had come over him? Why these thoughts of a woman who, if one was to believe the gossip, didn't give a damn for any man. She was a dried-up spinster with the temper and ways of a man. She was also the daughter of the man who'd murdered his father. The sooner he forgot all about her the better.

The trail now widened and there was the first faint whiff of humanity coming on the wind. He knew he wasn't many miles from Sweetwater. The smell of sewerage, horse manure and rotting garbage did not faze him. He was used to the smell of humanity from the days when he had been herded with other unwashed bodies in a dark, dank cell at night.

It was only when he smelled freedom and what it meant that he knew what real freedom was. To smell pine forests and greenery, and grass with the hot sun on it, and flowers he couldn't put a name to, made him realize what he'd missed for such a long part of his life. For all that he needed vengeance now.

He stopped beside a stream. It was evidently a popular camping-place for the signs were all there, trampled hoof-marks, wheel-ruts, the remains of dead fires and rubbish.

He took the mare to drink. On impulse, when she was done, he tied her to an overhanging tree-branch and stripped, leaving an untidy heap of dirty clothes on the bank.

As a cautionary measure he took his hand-gun and set it close by on a boulder that stood up from the water. Then he plunged in up to his waist, dousing his head and coming up to shake the drips from his tousled hair. By God, it felt good!

He kicked out and with powerful strokes of his arms he gained the other side of the stream. Chest heaving, he felt the heat of the mid-morning sun strike his back. This was good. It had been a long time since he'd relaxed like this. For once, life seemed to be a pleasure.

He dived again and again, playing like an otter, enjoying the coolness on sweated limbs. He decided he would cut his hair and beard while it was wet. At last, when he'd grown tired of his boyish antics, he prepared to leave the stream.

That was when he got a shock.

He was wading ashore and had just about made it when the sound of a horse's harness made him look up. He tripped on a sharp pebble in the water and then saw her sitting, cool as you please, on the back of a black gelding in the shadow of a shade tree. She was grinning but her features took on a more disapproving look when she saw he knew she was there.

'What in hell are you doing here?' he called furiously, and didn't even try to cover up. She'd already seen all there was to see.

'I came to water my horse! This is a public watering-place and I always stop here!'

'Hell's teeth! You could have given me some warning!'

'Why? I quite enjoyed the show! You're some swimmer, Mr Judd!'

'Thank you. Now would you mind turning your back so that I might get dressed?'

'Don't you think it's a little late for that? I'm quite happy where I am.'

He stared at her. She thought she had him at a disadvantage. He'd show her.

'You're no lady. A lady would be more discreet!'

'I'm no lady!'

'I can see that, so I'll just have to carry on doing what I intended doing.'

'And what was that?'

'I'm going to cut my hair and beard before

I dress. Do you mind?'

'Not at all.'

'Why don't you come down to the water and let your horse drink while we're talking?'

He stepped up on to the bank, and as she eased her horse forward she thought what a magnificent figure of a man he was. Wide strong shoulders, broad chest with a fuzz of black hair, long muscled legs also covered in faint black hairs, and as her eyes slid past his private parts she saw that they too were in proportion to this giant of a man. This man made her heart beat fast. For the first time in years she was attracted to a male and she couldn't even see his face!

She averted her eyes as the gelding moved past him to the water and so did not see him reach out and grab her by the waist. She was yanked off her saddle and tightly clasped before she knew what happened.

Then she kicked and tried to slap his face but an iron hand clutched her wrist and she saw the blue eyes laughing at her in the midst of black beard and shaggy hair.

Then he kissed her hard and she felt his hot lips on hers as his beard tickled her chin.

'You beast!' she shouted when at last he'd freed her lips.

'You asked for it … lady…' The hesitation over the word *lady* made her flush. It sounded so contemptuous.

'How dare you! Put me down at once!'

He raised heavy eyebrows.

'Now?'

'Yes, at once!' Her chest heaved with anger. His eyes watched the movement. She certainly looked and felt good at close quarters. He changed his mind about her being a dried-up spinster. She was ripe for the taking.

'Oh, very well.' He dropped her into the stream. She fell with a splash and a scream, thrashing about until she found her feet.

She spluttered and turned to curse him but he was walking up the bank, picking up his clothes. He began to dress; his haircut would have to wait for the barber after all.

Then, ready to ride, he laughed at her as she was trying to squeeze water out of her riding-pants and shirt.

'Why don't you strip 'em off and lay them out to dry in the sun? You could have a swim! Who knows, you might enjoy it as much as I did!' He waved a hand mockingly. As he rode away, he heard her shout after him:

'You bastard! We'll get you for this! Pa was right! You're a no-good son of a bitch!'

FOUR

Judd made for the hitching rail in front of the barber's establishment. It was sand-wiched conveniently between a hardware store selling guns and ammunition and a general store selling everything from food staples, pots and pans to clothes. Judd reckoned he should buy his new gear before putting himself in the hands of the barber.

He entered the general store and at once two elderly ladies dressed in black sniffed and moved their skirts so that there would be no contact. They quickly left the store.

The storeman, busy wrapping up a parcel of calico for a young mother, turned sharply to him.

'Itinerants not welcome here, mister. We don't give handouts!'

The young woman pulled her small child close to her skirts and looked frightened.

'I'm not an itinerant. I'm here as a customer. I take it my dough is as good as the sheriff's?'

'Aw, well, if you've got cash I'll be with you in a bit, but don't get too near my stock. I don't aim to fumigate the place after you've gone!'

Judd shrugged off the words. He'd been cussed and sworn at too long to make a fuss now. He knew he was a sight to frighten babies, but what the hell...

He moved amongst the racks of shirts and picked out an extra-large black wool flannel item and then moved on to the rows of denim pants.

Then he found the little man beside him.

'I'm afraid you cain't try 'em on.'

Judd looked down at him and grinned.

'I wasn't aimin' to, mister. Now I want underpants and a vest, some socks and a pair of your best riding-boots. Mine, as you see,' he lifted a foot to show the state of his scuffed and badly worn boots, 'need replacing.' He quietly withdrew his wad of notes and the man's eyes bulged. Judd knew what he was thinking.

'I'm no holdup merchant. I got this lot all legal and proper, so get moving, mister. I want to go next door for a bath and a haircut. So pronto it is!'

The little storekeeper scuttled away and found the biggest set of woollen underwear he could lay his hands on and some thick socks and boots.

'You'd better try the boots on for size. They're the biggest I stock.'

So Judd sat down and pulled off the worn-out boots. He peeled off socks stiff with sweat and with holes in toes and heels. He tried on the soft leather boots and sighed with relief.

'Yes, these are fine. I'll keep 'em on and I'll have another pair of these here socks. You can burn the others.'

The storeman turned his lips down at that.

'It will cost you.'

Judd sighed.

'All right. How much?'

'A dollar.'

'A dollar for burning my boots and socks?'

'Yes, well, you know how it is. I've got to hire a boy to build a fire hot enough to burn leather…'

'OK, I understand. What about throwing in a neckerchief as a sign of goodwill? I'm a good customer. I'm paying cash, not like some of your neighbours who put everything on the slate!'

'OK, you get a neckerchief. Pick which one you want.'

Judd chose a red-and-white one and added it to his pile.

'What about a new leather jacket? And by

the looks of that hat you need a new one to go with your new gear.'

Judd removed his greasy Stetson and handled it fondly.

'I guess you're right. It don't go with the new gear. I think a black one would be right for me. I'll try this one.' He jammed a large-brimmed Stetson on his head.

The storeman cringed and hoped it would fit. He didn't want all his men customers complaining that they got lice from old Pete's hats.

But Judd kept the hat on and finally paid up, a new black-leather jacket over one arm and a brown-paper parcel of his new gear in the other.

Then he strode into the barber's and stood with legs wide apart as he surveyed the surroundings.

The barber was in the midst of stropping his razor, his last customer having blunted it. He looked up and sighed. Here was another woolly-headed bastard who hadn't seen his face in a long time. These kind were hell to shave and cutting their matted hair was an act of sheer willpower, for fleas would be jumping all ways.

'How much for a bath, a haircut and a shave?'

'A dollar to you, but you'll have to join a queue for a bath. I only got two and the boy has to fill and empty each one before the next user.'

'Huh. Then you can cut and shave me while I wait.'

The barber's face lengthened.

'I usually cut hair after a bath. It'll cost you extra if I cut it now!'

'How much?'

'Another dollar for the inconvenience.'

'A dollar? That's highway robbery!'

The man's shoulders shrugged. 'Take it or leave it. It's up to you!'

'Throw in a bottle of that snake oil and you're on! It's good for killing nits, isn't it?'

'Yes, good for everything, but don't drink it. I did that once and I was on the privy for a week! OK. An extra dollar and I throw in a bottle!'

'Done!'

Later, Judd stared at his face. He hadn't seen it in years and a total stranger looked back at him from the mirror. He stroked his smooth jaw. It felt strange.

He'd aged from the boy he remembered, and the white below his cheekbones didn't match the tanned skin over his forehead. He reckoned he looked a sorry mess.

His head too felt cold. The barber had given him a close cut on account of the nits. He smelled strange too, of carbolic and lye soap.

'Jeeze ... I can't believe it! I look like someone going straight to hell!'

The barber grinned.

'You smell a damned sight better even though you haven't yet had your bath! Two ... three days and the sun will get rid of the piebald look. Now can I sell you a razor? I've got some new stock in. I can let you have one for two dollars!'

Judd laughed.

'You don't miss a trick! Go on, I'd better have one. I don't want the experience again that I've just gone through. Now what about that bath?'

An hour later Judd stepped out of the barber's and squinted into the sun. He felt good. His new clothes fitted him fairly well and though an aura of carbolic surrounded him, he was fast becoming used to it.

He strolled along the sidewalk towards the saloon. He could use a drink and if possible he could down a steak and brownies and maybe a piece of pumpkin pie if it was available.

He noticed that the womenfolk did not sniff or move away from him as they passed by. Yes, he was once more in the land of the living. He should have done this when he first came out of jail. But of course he hadn't had such a hunk of cash in his hand before.

Inside the saloon he saw the tables and sniffed cooking beef. He was in luck. This place must have a good cook.

He ordered a whiskey at the bar.

'What about grub! I want to eat.'

The barman waved him to one of the tables.

'We got roast beef and steaks, or pork chops, take your pick, all with fried potatoes and sweetcorn. We got peach pie for afters if you want it.'

'Give me a double portion of steak and fries and a double portion of pie. I'm a big feller to fill!'

'Right! Coming up as soon as the wife can dish it!' The man hurried off to give the order.

He was downing his second whiskey and brooding on how to come into contact with the old judge when the batwing doors opened and in walked Milly Burke. She strode over to the bar and ordered a beer.

He leaned back in his chair and tipped his hat to the back of his head so as to see her more clearly. She was wearing a new blue-checked shirt with the old dried riding-pants but her hat still looked damp. She looked to be in a bad temper, answering the barman's greeting snappily. She took a long swallow of beer and sighed. She ordered a pickled pork sandwich and a piece of pie. Then she took a cursory glance around the saloon. Her eyes flicked past Judd without recognition. Then his own meal was being served and he shifted slightly so that his back was to her.

The beef was good. His guts growled for good food and he concentrated on his stomach. He wanted no continued quarrel with that feisty bitch while he ate.

Then he heard the batwings slam. He looked round. Only her empty glass and dishes were there. The barman caught his eye and winked.

'Something bothering Miss Milly. In a right tizzy she was, but then, she's often kicking up a fuss over something or other.'

He leaned forward confidentially and looked at several customers sitting further away. Then he said softly:

'Mind you, I don't know how this town would do without her! Takes a bullet out of a man far better than the old doc. Her hand doesn't shake when she does it. I reckon she's seen more naked men in her life than my old woman's seen me in forty years of leg shackling!'

'You don't say?' Judd stiffened and his ears pricked up. No wonder she wasn't fazed when she caught him with his underpants off!

'Yeah … she never liked to see me naked, God rest her soul, nor me, her! Very prudish, my old woman.'

'Then who's cooking for you now?' Judd's head nodded to the kitchen door.

'Oh, that's her sister! She's a widow-woman and we have an arrangement.' The barman chuckled. 'I call her my wife to strangers!'

'Tell me about Miss Milly.'

'Nothing much to tell. Works and swears like a man, has no time for any sparking. Some of the boys have tried it and one stubborn fool nearly got his balls blown off! She's a rare one, is that. But she's got her good side. Helps old folks and kids. She made the mayor put pressure on the preacher to hold a hoedown in aid of the windows and orphans after the war was over and she was only a kid then. She lost her feller in the war. That and her pa's accident has made her what she is today.' Then he moved away to serve a cowman and his foreman who'd just breezed in off the street.

Judd finished his meal and ruminated on what he'd heard. Yes, he'd made his mind up. He'd get this business over and then he'd go back and take his chances at sparking Miss Milly.

He paid his dues, then casually asked the barman where the old retired judge, George Gannon, was now living. He'd heard he'd settled in these parts and he'd like to call on him for old times' sake.

'Sure. George Gannon came here about five years ago to live with a daughter and her family. They live a couple of miles out of town. You can't miss the Atherton place. Joe's Sarah's husband and they'll be right welcoming. Old George don't get many visitors these days. He's crippled with rheumatism and got a dodgy leg, so don't get into the saloon much these days. He'll be right glad to see you. He's a good talker is George!'

'Thank you. I'll give him your regards.'

'Yes, you do that and tell him if he wants a barrel of moonshine sending up, I'll see to it right quick!'

Outside in the strong sunlight Judd took a deep breath. He was a step nearer to what he'd hoped and dreamed of for so long. To face that son of a bitch judge and see the horror in his eyes before he pulled the trigger... His mind was made up. He'd deal with the judge first and then go after the Goodisons.

The mare whinnied as he unloosed her. He patted her neck as he leapt aboard.

'OK, old girl, you'll get your legs stretched as soon as we hit the trail. Now I wonder what Milly was doing in town?' he finished softly to himself.

He rode the length of Main Street, studying the houses and stores and saloons.

He reckoned this would be a high old place on Saturday nights when the crews of the surrounding ranches came into town for a booze-up and a woman.

He'd forgotten to ask his friendly barman in which direction was the Atherton place, so he stopped by a small boy and asked. The boy pointed east. Judd threw him a dime.

'Gee, thanks mister!' The boy grinned and ran straight to the store to spend it.

Judd kept the horse on a tight rein until he was well out of town. He didn't want to cause a sensation because once the old man was dead there would be hell to pay. He would have to be well out into the hills if he wanted to backtrack to the Goodison brothers' place.

He didn't care what happened to him after he'd finished his business with the Goodisons. He had to find out whether Luke had survived his bullet. He had to know. He couldn't rest otherwise.

He saw the sprawling one-storey white-painted house long before he reached the gate. It stood back surrounded by fruit trees. It stood on a little hill. He reckoned there would be marvellous views from the veranda, if you had the time to sit and stare.

He saw the hunched figure rocking gently in his chair and guessed it was the old judge himself. Judd felt his nerves tighten and his breath quickened. He'd never killed a man in cold blood. This time it would be murder.

He rode into the yard and dismounted below the veranda steps. He tossed the reins of the mare over the hitching rail and then leisurely climbed the steps. The rocking-chair stopped as the judge peered up at him with dim eyes.

'Remember me?'

'Should I?' The old man's legs moved as he strove to rise from his chair. A big hand pushed him back hard against the chairback.

'Does the name Matthew Judd ring a bell?'

For a long moment the old man just stared up at Judd and then his mouth dropped open.

'Judd! Were you that kid who got put away

for that bank robbery in Nashville?'

'The very one, Judge, and you put me there! Remember?'

The old man's head nodded slowly.

'Why are you here now?' he asked quietly, although beads of sweat were breaking out on his brow. Judd couldn't but feel a kind of admiration for him. He had guts, had the old feller.

'You know why I'm here, Judge. I'm the one going to dispense justice now! You owe me twenty years of my life. I kind of want to take several years of your life in exchange!'

George Gannon swallowed, his mouth suddenly dry. He was having a hard time not to shake.

'So what are you waiting for? Go on, do it if you've got the balls to kill an old man in cold blood. Go on, do it!' His voice rose to a shriek.

Judd drew his gun, steeling himself to do what he'd dreamed of for so many years. This was the moment he'd been waiting for.

'I wouldn't do it if I was you,' a woman's

voice said grimly behind him, 'or I'll put daylight right through your back!'

Judd stiffened.

'Drop the gun, buster, right now!'

Judd reckoned the feisty bitch would do exactly what she said.

Then he half-turned.

'OK, Miss Burke. There'll always be another day.' He smiled mockingly at her. 'What are you doing here?'

'You!' She was so startled she nearly dropped her gun.

'Yes, it's me.' He stooped casually, picked up the Peacemaker and holstered it as another young woman with frightened eyes and a baby in her arms came round the corner of the house.

'Is everything all right, Milly?'

'Yes, Sarah. This is the Matthew Judd I was telling you about, the man who won the rodeo competition. The big wild man who seems to have cleaned himself up!' She frowned at him. 'What are you going to do now?'

88

Judd shrugged. 'It seems that the business between the judge and me will have to be resumed later. I'll bid you ladies good day.'

'Where are you going?' Milly asked sharply.

'I have business with the Goodisons. Don't worry. I'll be back!' He ran down the steps, unloosed his mare's reins and mounted. He raised his hat to them all and turned to the old man.

'This is your lucky day, Judge. Next time might not be so lucky!' He turned to ride away.

'Wait!'

He checked the mare at the sound of Milly's voice and waited while she came near the nervously stepping horse.

'Are you going to the Goodison place?'

He smiled. 'You think I'm a fool?'

'It doesn't matter what I think of you. I only wanted to tell you that the Goodison brothers' crew is made up of professional gunmen. Luke Goodison is obsessed by land. He wants all the small ranchers out and to take over all the territory.'

'Then he'll want your place too. Your father is going to have a mighty battle on his hands unless Luke Goodison is stopped.' Judd stared into the distance, then looked at Milly. 'I don't know whether Luke Goodison is dead or alive. I must find out.'

'Why do you say that?'

'Because he and his brother bushwhacked me on the way into town. The last time I saw him he was out cold on the trail.'

'You shot him?'

'Yes, but I could have just winged him.'

The tension seemed to leave Milly. She put her gun away. 'If you've killed him you got my thanks and those of the rest of our community, and if he's wounded, then at least it gives us some time. Thank you.'

'You're welcome, ma'am.' With that, Judd rode away. Milly stared after him. Then she went up the steps. She stood before the old man, hand on hip.

'Why was Judd going to kill you?'

'Milly … please, Pa's had a shock.' Sarah

tried to pull Milly away. The baby started to cry. Milly looked at her friend, seeing the distress and fear in her face.

'Sarah, go inside and see to Billy. I've got to know about Judd. Now go!'

Sarah, struck afresh by the urgency in Milly's voice, obeyed. Milly waited until the screen door clanged behind them and she and the old man were alone.

'Now tell me about Judd.'

George Gannon's mouth set stubbornly.

'It's none of your business. It all happened a long time ago.'

Milly sighed. 'Why is it that old men like you and Pa think it right to tell a woman it's none of her business! If I was a man you'd tell me!'

'That would be different,' the old judge said sulkily. 'But you're not and I think there's nothing worse than a female who doesn't know her place in life! You're spoiled, Milly and I've told your pa over and over again that he's too soft with you! If I was him, I'd have had you married off years ago! You need breaking in, my girl before it's too late!'

'How about you minding your own business? How dare you talk to me like that? All I'm asking is why was Judd here and why was he all set to shoot you! If it wasn't for me, you'd be dead meat now! So come on and tell me what I want to know. I'm not going from here until I hear the truth, so help me God!'

'You're a stubborn wild she-cat, that's what you are, and I'm sorry for your poor father!'

'You can call me what you like! I don't care a snap!'

Old George sighed.

'Can't we have a beer first?'

'No. I'll not let Sarah come to you until I know what I want to know. I'm warning you...'

Suddenly he was angry.

'All right, you bitch, you can have it straight! More than twenty years ago Matthew Judd took the rap for a bungled bank robbery. He was there in the bank as a customer. There was a fight and Judd got knocked out after Luke Goodison robbed the bank vault. He and his brother got away because of my deputy but not before Luke stuffed a bundle of notes into Judd's trousers. He woke up in jail and the deputy testified that Judd was one of the bank robbers. I knew different, for Luke came to me the night of the robbery and, God help me, he bribed me with ten thousand dollars to keep him and Jonas out of it. I needed the dough at that time. I had gambling debts and had been threatened with exposure. You couldn't have a judge exposed as a gambler who didn't pay up!'

'So you and the deputy railroaded Judd and he took the rap?'

'Yep. We reckoned a kid like him was just a saddle tramp anyway.'

'And you gave him twenty years? What happened to the deputy?'

'Got killed in a fight in a saloon. I reckoned Luke Goodison set him up but I had no proof so I kept my mouth shut.' His eyes lowered at Milly's accusing stare. 'I've never felt right, ever since. It's always haunted me.'

'And so it should,' she said with contempt.

'You'll not tell Sarah and Joe? They know nothing about it.'

'Why open a can of worms now? It would do no good and I think you'll have enough to worry about when Judd comes back!'

'*If* he comes back! Luke Goodison's place is brimming over with pros itching for a fight!'

Milly smiled. 'I don't think he'll go in with all guns firing. I think he'll stalk his targets if I'm any judge of the guy.'

George Gannon gave her a sly glance.

'Has he taken your fancy, Milly?'

She reared up indignantly. 'Of course not! Don't be ridiculous!'

She stalked off into the kitchen and slammed the screen door behind her but she still heard the old man's laughter.

FIVE

Luke Goodison sat propped up in bed, his right arm swathed in bandages. He glowered at his brother, Jonas.

'So you and the boys found no sign of him? Goddammit, I should have been out there myself! Call yourselves trackers! A blind donkey could have done better!'

Jonas flushed. 'We did our best, Luke. We split up and hunted in all directions.'

'And all messed up his trail, no doubt! It's time I was up and doing the job myself!' Painfully he tried to rise, cursing as he did so.

'Now take it easy, Luke, or you'll start the bleeding again. You're lucky to be alive, so don't do anything rash!'

Luke gave him a hard, piercing look.

'You like the idea of me being stuck here, don't you, Jonas? I've seen the way you look at me … you and Buster. You both think I don't know.'

'Know what, Luke?'

'That you're itching to take over the ranch, you and Buster. I've seen you with your heads together … plotting … and one of these days you're going to go too far!'

'Are you threatening us, Luke? For if you are I might be sorry I dragged you back to the ranch. You owe me your life, Luke, and don't forget it!'

Luke was jolted with surprise. Jonas standing up to him? He didn't sound like the meek and mild Jonas who did his bidding with sick-making eagerness to please. What had come over him? Or was it because he, Luke, was lying helpless in bed? He glowered.

'It's time I was up and doing, so get out while Billy here helps me to dress.'

Jonas looked from Luke to the silent youth waiting in the corner of the room. Billy was Luke's whipping-boy and took his bullying without complaint. Billy reminded him of himself and he wanted to puke. He detested Billy for what he was.

'OK, Luke. Have it your own way, damn you!' He walked out of the bedroom, slamming the door behind him.

Outside, Buster waited.

'Sounds like he was as stubborn as usual,' Buster said carefully.

'Yes. Let's get outside and then we can talk. That snivelling Billy might be listening behind the door.'

Outside in the yard the two brothers looked at each other.

'Well?' Buster waited, trying to read Jonas's expression.

'He suspects something's up. The son of a bitch has the instincts of a jaguar.'

'So? What does he know?'

'Nothing, but he suspects. He's going out there himself. He thinks we haven't got a brain cell between us.'

'We can't afford a range war, Jonas. If we go hunting that Judd feller in a pack the ranchers will think we're all out for a take-over. Luke brought in too many professional gunmen. The townsfolk and the ranchers are just waiting for a signal to band together and fight. It's that Burke bitch who keeps them on edge.'

'You should have sparked her, Buster, when Luke suggested it and then we wouldn't have this situation now, but you wouldn't have none of her, remember?'

Buster didn't answer. He remembered well enough. Unbeknown to Jonas and Luke he had sparked her at one of the hoedowns years ago and she'd laughed at him and made some insulting remark about rather being found in bed with a pig. He'd hated her ever since.

Then he said softly:

'Why didn't you spark her yourself? Or were you too besotted with that tart in the saloon who ran away with that gambling feller?'

Jonas, in turn, was silent. Betsy had been a sore point with him. Hell! If only he'd had real cash of his own, then Betsy might have stayed. They could even have married. Luke was to blame for all that. He kept both him and Buster on a tight rein. They weren't much better off than the cowboys who worked for them.

'I suppose I'm like you. I couldn't face looking at Milly Burke over the breakfast table for the rest of my life!'

They both laughed and did not see Luke watching them from his window.

Judd rode down Main Street in Sweetwater and tethered his horse outside the general store. He nodded to several passersby who thought they recognized him from the rodeo but he did not stop to chat. He had in his head a list of things he needed and didn't want to be distracted.

Inside the store the storekeeper recognized him for the man who paid cash. He rubbed his hands together and came forward eagerly, leaving a woman examining several bales of cloth.

'Hi! Come back for some more shirts?'

'Nope. I want a sack of coffee, a small sack of flour, some beans and some pickled belly-pork.'

'Yes sir! Coming up right away, sir!'

'Oh, and I want a box of lucifers and toss in some of that there sugar candy.'

He prowled around the store while the order was made up, picking out a wad of bandaging and bottle of iodine, just in case he needed them. Lead poisoning could be the very devil.

Then he saw what the Indians called a parfleche, a leather-sewn sack with a draw-string. He bought that to hang over the pommel of his horse.

The staples were packed inside and Judd was ready to ride and camp out for several days.

The storekeeper watched him ride away, wondering what the big man had in mind, then he went back to his lady customer and persuaded her that the dark-blue silk would be fine for a going-to-church dress.

Judd hummed as he left Sweetwater. His

intention was to lie low and watch the Goodison ranch. He wanted to catch Luke Goodison if he was still alive and face him before shooting him again. He wanted to see the fear in the man's eyes. Then he would turn his attention on Jonas. The younger brother, Buster, he had no interest in. He'd been but a child when the robbery had taken place.

He circled the ranch and the buildings from a distance, stopping frequently to use the spyglass he'd won from an army veteran at a poker-game. Now it was coming in useful.

He watched the genuine cowboys at work and counted the professional gunmen who tended to lounge about idly together. Luke Goodison wouldn't approve of that if he was alive. He saw Jonas and Buster talking together in the yard and followed their movements when they approached the lounging men. He saw them listening to Jonas. Then they all made for their horses. They were going out on the hunt!

He smiled to himself. Were they hunting him or were they going after some poor rancher? It would be interesting to find out.

He watched them ride away south. He could follow at leisure. Now he wanted to know if Luke was still around. He moved closer to the ranch, leaving his mare tethered beneath a stand of trees.

He found a niche in between an outcrop of stone, lay down on his belly and waited. He had a good view of the front of the house.

It wasn't long before a man was being helped by a young boy to come outside on to the veranda. Judd's heart leapt. It was Luke Goodison. There was no mistaking him. He looked the same as he'd done that day of the robbery, only more grizzled and heavier. He wore a bandage around his shoulder. So, the bastard had been lucky. Judd had aimed for his head.

He was tempted to shoot him there and then. The rifle beside him was loaded and ready to fire. But he didn't want that. He wanted Goodison to realize that his destiny had caught up with him.

He inched forward so that he could see

better. That was when a couple of birds took flight from a tree close by. Goodison looked up, startled. Judd lay still, then risked a peek. Goodison was making his way painfully into the yard and the youth was running to the corral close by to capture Goodison's horse. Was the fool going to ride out after his men? It looked very much like it. Judd watched with interest. This could be the break he needed. He could follow Goodison and confront him before he met up with his men! Judd could have laughed aloud and bellied backwards to get to his mare and be ready to ride.

But before he'd backed off a couple of yards he heard the drumming of hoofs. He cursed. It sounded like the return of the posse.

Judd watched as Jonas, followed by Buster and the gunmen, came into the yard at a gallop but what got Judd rare and mad was that Jonas and Buster had Milly Burke between them. Jonas was holding a leading-rein and it looked as if Milly's wrists were tied to the pommel of her horse.

She looked as if they'd roughed her up. She'd lost her hat, her hair hung about her shoulders and the new blue shirt was torn. His first impulse was to go in with both guns blazing, but he knew that would be folly with the other men close by.

He heard Luke Goodison bellow at his brothers.

'What in hell's been going on?'

Judd saw Jonas laugh but couldn't hear what was said. Then he heard Luke roar:

'You fools! You'll have the whole range up in arms! Goddammit! Don't you ever use your brains?'

Jonas looked angry. He was being made a fool of in front of the men. He saw Buster looking sulky. He wondered if his brother would tell the truth or let him, Jonas, take the brunt of Luke's anger. Buster remained silent. With a look of contempt at Buster, Jonas gave a run-down on what had happened.

'Burke's foreman and his men were rounding up mustangs and the son of a bitch thought we were raiding them. Latimer fired first. He hit O'Grady and Buster here, put one in Latimer and then all hell broke loose! We was in the middle of a fight! Then this here bitch came from nowhere, fighting mad. She laid low Jenkins before we knew she was there! Buster got her in the end, not without a struggle, and here she is!'

'And what in hell are you going to do with her?'

'We're gonna take her back to Jim Burke, me and Buster here, and the boys are with us in this.'

Luke slowly glared around at the waiting men.

'You taking orders from him?'

The men looked shifty-eyed but determined. They all looked at each other, not sure whose side to take. Luke Goodison was the real leader, after all, and the pay from him had been good, but Jonas had offered better odds if they followed him.

'Come on, one of you speak up! You're supposed to be tough, the best, so who's going to back up this piece of shit!'

'Listen, boss,' one of the older men began, 'we're professionals. We go with the man who offers the best deal. Jonas here aims to take over the Burke ranch and he's offered us all a piece of the action!'

Luke took a deep breath, his arm paining him badly. If he'd been a fit man he would have shot both his brothers, he was in such a rage. He turned to Jonas and Buster, ignoring the silent girl between them.

'You mean to tell me you were going in there to dicker with Jim Burke and expect him to turn over his ranch just like that?'

'He would when he saw a gun poking into his daughter's side!'

Luke laughed and the brothers flushed with anger, for it was the laughter of a man who humoured two small boys.

'Neither of you would have the guts to shoot her!' he mocked.

Buster eased his mount forward until he was directly in front of Luke.

'You've never really seen me, have you,

Luke? You've always regarded me as the baby who has to be told every step of the way. I've gone along with it for the sake of peace but it's over, Luke! Jonas and me are taking over Jim Burke's place, not sharing it with you or anybody else.' He looked at the men behind him. 'These fellers are going to help us! We're all sick of your ways, Luke! There's better ways of acquiring land than just scaring off small ranchers and making enemies! It's time to move on and become respectable. I aim to do just that.'

'And how do you mean to do that if you kill the girl?'

'It won't come to that, Luke. I reckon Jim Burke thinks too much of Milly to let that be a possibility.'

Suddenly Buster saw a grudging respect in Luke's eyes, coupled with the smouldering anger. He smiled. It was the first time ever that he'd seen that look.

Luke tried to flex his bandaged arm.

'You want to thank your lucky stars this arm's bandaged! If I could, brothers or not,

I'd shoot you both for mutiny!'

'If that's the case, Luke, maybe I should finish what Judd started!'

Luke reared up, back straight. He couldn't believe what he was hearing.

'You wouldn't dare!'

'Wouldn't I? You always insisted I was a yellow-streaked, brainless idiot! You dead, Luke, would mean Jonas taking over the ranch and me taking over Jim Burke's place. That way we can end the bitterness on the range!'

'Why you...' Luke struggled clumsily to grab his gun with his left hand. His eyes widened as he saw Buster's gun come up and aim at his head. 'Buster!' he bellowed just before his baby brother fired. Everyone present was stunned with the swiftness of it.

Buster turned to a white-faced Jonas, holding his smoking gun.

'Aren't you going to thank me, big brother, for giving you a ranch on a plate?'

Neither of them saw the look of horror on Milly Burke's face or the set of her determined lips. She had seen something she would never forget as long as she lived. A new hate for the Goodison brothers smouldered inside and took root.

Judd watched the whole proceedings with interest. He would have given anything to have been an ant, listening in to the conversation. He wondered why the young Goodison had ended it with the shooting of his brother. It sounded very much like trouble in the camp.

He regretted the shooting. Buster had robbed him of the pleasure of facing Luke Goodison and seeing the fear in his eyes before he died. Still, Buster had done a good job. Now there was only Jonas to attend to before he went back to visit the old judge.

He rubbed his bristly chin. It itched in this heat and it reminded him that he must use his new razor or else he'd soon have a thick beard once again.

He watched the bunch of men ride out with Milly still tied to her horse. He figured they were going to the Burke ranch to face Jim Burke. He had a good idea what this was all about. They either wanted cash for Milly, or they wanted land. Maybe young Buster figured on forcing Milly to marry him. Somehow that thought enraged him, no matter how stubborn a bitch she was.

He let the bunch of men get a clear start, then followed, keeping to the high country so that he could watch their progress through his spyglass.

Yes, they were heading for the Burke ranch. Now this was a new game entirely, with new rules. What he had to figure now was whether to go ahead and shoot Jonas out of hand or go in there and rescue Milly. Which was his priority? Rescuing Milly robbed him of surprise when he went after Jonas. The bastard would have all his men on the watch for him.

Coolly he considered the odds. Milly won. He'd have to figure a way of getting to her. Then he remembered his new identity. Jonas and Buster wouldn't recognize him as Judd, the man who'd won the rodeo competition. He could ride in to Burke's place in all innocence with the notion of asking for a job.

He must get that shave forthwith!

A couple of hours' ride from Jim Burke's spread, the bunch of men stopped. Milly was allowed to step into the bushes with Buster standing by with his rifle at the ready for fear she might make a break. The men built a fire, brewed coffee and ate what there was in their saddle-bags.

Judd took the time to do likewise and also to shave, having camped near a small stream. Then he packed everything away for a quick start should there be any signs that they were moving on.

Suddenly he was alerted by a shot. Peering through his spyglass he saw that the men lounging around a small fire were also surprised. They sprang to their feet in alarm, grabbing for their guns.

Searching the landscape with the glass he saw a flurry of birds rise squawking as if panicking from what was happening below.

Then he saw a figure crashing through the thick scrub. Another shot was fired and he swore. The glimpse he had of the fleeing figure was that of Milly Burke. He saw her stagger and then run on. At once he unloosed his horse and cut through the straggly bushes on to hard ground. He galloped down the steep incline in a course that would intercept her.

It seemed an age before he caught up with her. Riding hard, he bent, caught her under the arms and lifted her on to the saddle in front of him. Out of the corner of his eye he saw Buster Goodison, limping behind, his rifle at his shoulder and a murderous look on his face. He spurred the mare to greater speed and the shot that came missed by a couple of feet. He heard the angry buzz, as of a hornet, and the bullet went crashing into the undergrowth.

Grimly he rode on, conscious of the panting sweaty woman slumped against him. No words were spoken. It was as if she was now barely conscious.

Up on the slopes one more, he brought the mare to an easy canter, looking for a good place to halt. He found it near the very stream he'd stopped at before. There was a cluster of rocks close by. He and Milly could hide, but it would not be so easy to hide the mare, for she was nervous of dark enclosed spaces.

The mare quivered and hung her head, sides heaving after carrying a double load. He dismounted, Milly clinging to the mare's mane. Then he pulled her gently into his arms and carried her to lie between two boulders. Then, patting and gentling the mare, he led her into a crevice of rock and tethered her closely so that she couldn't back out. She protested, but he was firm with her and after talking quietly to her for a few minutes, she became calm and stood still.

Then Judd came and crouched over Milly, who was now stirring and blinking her eyes.

'You all right?'

She struggled up on one elbow.

'I ... I think so. I suddenly felt faint. I've

never fainted in my life before!' she said, a little defiantly as if he would think her a poor helpless creature.

'That's understandable. I saw you running like a deer through the undergrowth. I'll get you some water.'

'I'd rather have some whiskey. You don't have any, by any chance?'

He smiled down at her. She was some tough woman!

'As a matter of fact I do. I never go anywhere without it.' He crawled away to get his bottle from his saddle-bag.

He returned and handed the bottle to her.

'You'll have to drink out of the bottle.'

She smiled. 'I've done that before!'

He raised his eyebrows.

'You pride yourself on being one of the boys. It doesn't suit you, if you don't mind me saying so!'

She looked at him squarely into those twinkling blue eyes.

'I don't care a damn what you think,' she lied.

'So we know how we stand. What happened out there?'

'Those bastards the Goodisons bushwhacked us. One of our men, Nickie, took a shot at them and all hell broke loose. I saw it all. I was coming in with a stray. Nickie was shot…' she hesitated a little, then, lifting her head high, she said defiantly, 'I think I killed a man.' She glared at Judd, daring him to make a comment. He shrugged his shoulders and said offhandedly:

'Then you weren't smart enough. You got caught and hauled back to Luke as a trophy and he got himself shot!'

She started. 'How do you know all that?'

'I was watching. I saw them head out with you and figured they were taking you back to your father for ransom, and I followed you all. How come you were running hell for leather away from Buster?'

'When we camped, he untied me so that I could go into the bushes.' Again she glared at Judd, daring him to make a remark. 'When I came out he left me loose so that I could eat. We talked, at least he talked and I listened. Some rubbish about marrying and ending the range war. I just listened and kinda went along with him just to calm him down. But I think I give out the wrong message... After a while the bastard got excited and pulled me into the bushes. I tried to yell but he put a hand over my mouth and as we were a little distance away from the others, I don't think they noticed.'

'Then what happened?' Judd's anger was rising. Buster had never been a target for his revenge but now it was a different matter.

'He tried to ... to ... er...'

'Rape you?' Judd asked brutally.

'Yes, but I kicked and fought him and I bit his lip when he tried to kiss me. Then he got me on the ground and I kicked him between the legs and he rolled away, groaning horribly, and then I grabbed a piece of dead wood and hit him over the head!'

'Good girl! You sure do have grit!'

'Then I ran away as fast as I could and now I'm here with you!'

'Just so! Now, the problem is, what am I going to do with you?'

She looked surprised.

'You'll take me home, of course!'

'I wasn't figuring on going back to face your father.'

'But you must! He'll be grateful.'

'You think so? You think he'll be grateful to the man whose father he killed and as far as he knows, might be gunning for him?'

'Then I'll walk as soon as I get my strength back. I'll not be beholden to you!'

'And get yourself caught again by the Goodison mob? If I was a betting man I'd say the odds are on them riding in and stringing your father up!'

'Then what should I do, just sit here?'

'No. I figure we should make for the nearest neighbour and alert the whole range. How many ranchers can you count on?'

'Let's see … seven or eight small ranchers and about as many dirt farmers. Then there's the townsfolk. The Goodisons have never been popular. They and their men have a reputation for causing mayhem every time they ride into town.'

'So, we ride to the nearest neighbour, sound the alarm and get a posse together. Then we go after the Goodisons once and for all.'

She gave him a guarded look.

'Are you going to tell me about you and the Goodisons?'

'Maybe some day, when the time is right. The priority now is getting you to somewhere safe and raising a posse. I'll take a look around, see if it's all clear, then we'll make for the nearest ranch.'

He scrambled away. Milly watched his tall muscular figure climb the highest boulder and lie crouched as he swept the area with his spyglass. Then he was slipping and sliding down fast.

'No sign of them. They must have ridden on to your spread. I think we'd better get going while we can. Can you walk? Or should I carry you to the mare?'

'I can walk,' she said snappily. 'I'm no

helpless female!'

'Suit yourself.' He strode off to untie and lead out the mare. He waited until Milly reached him, his face inscrutable. Then, without a word, he heaved her in front of the saddle and sprang up behind her.

She felt an iron arm holding her around the waist and, leaning back, was aware of his warmth and musky male scent. They did not speak as they rode away, except for Milly to give directions to Ed Summers' place.

SIX

Jim Burke was furious. He would have given anything to be able to stand up and blast that grinning bastard, Buster Goodison, in the face with his old shotgun. But he was helpless and his houseboy standing behind his chair smelled as if he'd crapped himself.

Four of his men were being herded into

the yard and a couple of gunnies were handling their weapons menacingly. The first man to move aggressively would surely get shot. The rest of his men were out on the range doing their usual chores. Even his housekeeper had been dragged outside and tied to a wagon wheel.

'So there you have it,' gloated Buster. 'We got your daughter and shot up your crew. Don't reckon they'll be coming back, Burke. They're all out there, dead as mutton! Now are you going to do the sensible thing and transfer your deeds to me, all legal-like and proper, or do you want to play it the hard way? It's up to you.'

'The deeds are not here. They're in the bank,' Burke replied gruffly, 'and I'd want proof Milly's still alive.' He was quick to see the look Jonas, who'd not said a word during this confrontation, gave to Buster. The look puzzled Burke. How come it was Buster and not Jonas or Luke who was running this show, and what about Milly? His reference about her being alive had brought forth a response from the silent Jonas.

Suddenly Jim Burke was a very frightened man.

'You bastards! If anything's happened to Milly, I'll see you swing for it!' he yelled in uncontrollable rage and fear.

Buster laughed. It wasn't good to hear and all who heard it tensed up. It sounded like the laughter of a madman.

'As a crippled old has-been, how do you think you're going to do that, eh? You mind your tongue, mister, or we'll string you up like a side of beef! Now about those deeds–'

'I told you, they're in the bank!' The words were spoken low as if all the stuffing had been squeezed out of Burke. His head hung low on his chest and his breathing was laboured.

'So! Jonas, take a look inside and find some paper and a pen. Scratch out a message to the bank manager that the deeds of one James Burke be dispatched by said messenger to the ranch forthwith. Now hurry, Jonas. You can be the messenger and the rest of you men can relax meanwhile. Maybe we'll find some liquor and we can do some celebrating while we wait!'

The men cheered, then their leader spoke up.

'What about these guys? We can't hold 'em up all day!'

'Jeeze! Do I have to tell you everything? Tie 'em up in the barn, and the woman too. Then we can drink in peace!'

There were loud cheers and the men went about their business, not without a few scuffles as Burke's men tried to defend themselves. Bruised and bloody, they were herded into the barn and tied to iron hooks in the walls.

One man glared at their captors.

'By God, when I get free I'll get you, you bastards!'

The answer was a kick in the face.

'You're lucky to be alive!' growled the man fastening his wrists, 'so keep quiet, damn you!'

There was a short wait while Jonas went

into the house and rummaged around Burke's small office until he found what he needed, a sheet of paper and pen and ink. He scrawled with laboured writing the message Buster had suggested and then brought pen and ink and the paper out for Burke to sign, along with a small Bible on which to rest the paper.

'Here you are, old man. Here's the Bible, it might make you feel better. Sign the paper now, and you'll be OK.'

There was no response from Burke; his head hung still. Jonas nudged him impatiently.

'Come on now, don't be stubborn. Sign!' He gave him a harder nudge. Slowly Burke slipped sideways, hanging over the arm of his chair. Jonas looked at him stupidly, then slowly touched him. He looked up at the watching Buster. 'By God, the old bastard's foxed us! He's dead!'

Buster swore and dismounted, throwing the reins to one of the watching men. He strode across to the figure slumped in the wheelchair and roughly pulled his head back. Dead eyes stared up at him.

'The old goat's had a heart attack!'

Now Buster didn't know what to do. His new-found confidence deserted him. This new development was past his reckoning. He flung back the head and swore again. He turned savagely to Jonas.

'This is all your fault! You said it would be a good idea to go it alone. You said it would be easy!'

Jonas threw away the Bible and the paper and lashed out at Buster, catching him a glancing blow to the jaw.

'Shut up, Buster! You're becoming hysterical! We just take over the ranch house, and we wait for the girl and whoever she brings with her! We'll fight it out!'

'And what about the Lazy S, you fool? Do we fight it out here and maybe lose the Lazy S? Have you thought of that?'

Jonas looked baffled.

'We can't split our forces and defend both places. Let's get out of here and head for home! We can finish this business another day!'

Buster laughed wildly.

'Not before we fire the place! Come on, boys, we're gonna do this place over! Let those horses out of the corral and then fire the buildings!'

'What about the men and the woman in the main barn?' one of the gunmen called.

Buster shrugged and leapt aboard his horse.

'Let the bastards burn!'

Soon there were the sounds of terrified horses galloping away down the trail as fire and smoke engulfed the ranch and the buildings surrounding it.

The men rode away. Buster stopped on the brow of the hill and watched the flames and smoke rise up into the sky.

'That'll teach that stubborn proud bitch to laugh at me?' he muttered to himself. Then he turned and rode away after the others.

It didn't take Ed Summers long to grasp the situation after Judd and Milly rode into his yard. He was an ex-goldminer turned small rancher after an accident when he'd lost his left hand. He now had a hook attached to the stump by a leather thong and it was amazing what he could do with it. He owed Jim Burke much more than a favour. In the first place Jim had set Ed up with several cows, a bull and a stallion, and several broken-in mares, and later had included Ed's sellable horses with his own. Ed had been eternally thankful to Jim Burke for all his help.

Now he was raging mad at the thought of what Milly had gone through. He sent riders to the two ranches close by, with instructions to pass on the message for all to assemble at Ed Summers' place for an all-out war against the Goodisons, to deal with them once and for all. It was fighting talk.

Judd chafed at the delay. He was the outsider and had his own personal plan of campaign. Now that Milly was involved, it made it doubly important for him to end this twenty-year feud.

He ate with Ed Summers and his family with Milly and then, when the meal was over, said shortly, avoiding Milly's eyes:

'Ed, I want some grub. Enough for two days. I'm going on to the Lazy S to take a look around, spy out the land. Will you do that for me?'

Ed looked at Judd and then at Milly. He sensed that this man was something special to the woman.

'Of course, but wouldn't it be better if you waited and we all rode together? Milly can stay here with my wife and…'

'No!' said Milly furiously, 'don't treat me like some weak female! This is to do with me and my father! I have a right to come along and do whatever I can!'

Judd sighed and turned sharply to her.

'Stop it, you silly woman! This isn't the time to show how sassy you are! How in hell are we to face those goddamned gunmen of the Goodisons if we're worrying about you getting your fool head shot off! Now I'm telling you right now, you're staying with Ed's wife, or Ed and the others don't ride. Right?'

Ed Summers and his wife held their breaths. No one in living memory, except maybe Milly's pa, had ever spoken to Milly like that.

Milly never said a word but stood up from the table and hurried out on to the veranda. There was a pause, then Ed said softly to his wife,

'Go after her, love.'

When they were alone, Ed said quietly:

'I'll see you get the grub. When are you lighting out?'

'Right now. I'll take it easy. The mare's rested up and she's good for several hours yet. I'll take a look around and I'll be looking out for you. Bring some dynamite with you, if you've got some?'

Ed nodded. 'We got a stack. We've been clearing land of tree roots. You reckon to blow up the ranch?'

Judd laughed. 'Maybe. It all depends, but blowing up one of the buildings would shock 'em and give us an advantage. We'll play it as it comes!'

Ed Summers was thoughtful as Judd rode away. The man hadn't sought out Milly before leaving. If Milly had a sneaky fondness for the feller, she was going to have a tough time. He grinned a little. It would be interesting to watch the outcome. Meanwhile, he had more serious things to think about. He called up his men and gave his orders. Soon there would be the neighbours coming in and they must be ready to ride.

Night had fallen when Judd came within watching distance of the Lazy S ranch. Lights were flashing far down below, yells were echoing and shots were being fired. It sounded like mayhem, or could it be a drunken orgy? The moon was high and the landscape was bathed in silvery light which turned shadows blue. Judd tethered the mare well away from the spread, for the rattle of harness or a nicker from the mare could carry on the night air. There was the howl of a wolf in the distance but there were no growling animal hunters, only the sound of human predators.

Judd crept closer. He was now so near that he had to take each step with care for fear of guards around the place. Surely after what had happened at the Burke ranch they must realize that there would be repercussions?

But he could detect no guards. The Goodisons must believe they were all-powerful, that their reputation for having a strong professional crew would frighten off any reprisals. Or was it that Buster and Jonas couldn't control their men? That the men themselves were celebrating and to hell with what the brothers wanted? It was an intriguing puzzle.

Under another spate of gunfire he watched a couple of lurching cowboys shooting into the sky, aiming at a Stetson already pock-marked with holes. So that was it. It was a drunken orgy, and it looked as if Buster approved, for he came out of the ranch house waving a bottle in the air and giving the old rebel yell.

'Yeee ... ooo ... ouhhh!' ending with a

whoop. He fell down the veranda steps and sprawled on to the ground. He laughed and, raising the bottle to his lips, emptied it and threw it away before struggling to his feet.

The Goodison housekeeper suddenly erupted from the front door, laughing and waving a gun with a drunken man close behind her. He slapped her and the gun went off, a bullet whining into the night sky. Then he grabbed her as she squealed and her legs thrashed about as he tried to get her indoors again.

Judd watched with interest. There was no fear of the men going on a night raid tonight!

Judd wondered where Jonas was during the mayhem. If he could locate him, his own problem was solved. He gave a wolfish grin. If there was a god up there looking down, let him send Jonas Goodison to him!

He moved around cautiously, coming ever nearer to the homestead. He saw that the men were divided into two groups. Presumably the *pistoleros* and the cowmen kept to their own groups. They didn't even bunk together. There was a party going on in the barn and Judd reckoned that was where the pros lived and ate and slept, while the official bunkhouse with its own kitchen was left for the original crew.

He watched, estimating how much dynamite it would take to blow up the barn. That would give the gun-toting bastards something to think about! Judd had a very low opinion of men who hired out their guns for money. They had no loyalty to anyone but themselves.

He wondered how long it would be before Ed Summers and his men arrived. He watched the sky for the first sign of false dawn. Things were quietening down. He reckoned many of them would have passed out. Then he saw Jonas Goodison come staggering out of the barn. He stopped and urinated against the rough pine logs that made up the wall of the barn.

This was the moment he was waiting for!

He watched Jonas fumble with his pants

and come stumbling, singing softly, towards the house. Then he laughed quietly to himself in a curiously high tone and it triggered a forgotten memory in Judd's brain. He'd heard that laugh before!

Then it came to him in a flash of understanding. He'd heard that reckless laugh when he'd been out cold on the floor of that bank! He'd tried desperately to open his eyes but could not. As he'd sunk deeper into unconsciousness that laugh had been one of the last things he'd registered.

So he reckoned it must have been Jonas who'd stuffed that wad of notes down his pants. He'd reckoned it was a good joke. Now he was going to face the consequences of that joke!

Judd stepped out in front of him. All around was just darkness, only the moon's rays to see by. There were only the two of them astir. Legs apart, Judd stood his ground.

'Jonas Goodison! Remember me, Matthew Judd?'

The laughter ceased and Jonas looked up owlishly, belching a little. He seemed to have a hard job focusing his eyes. He screwed his face up to stare at Judd.

'So you finally found me! You're that green-horn kid way back in Nashville. Sure, I remember you. Luke said to watch out for you before ... before–'

'Buster shot him! He robbed me of the satisfaction of killing him.'

Jonas stiffened his back with an effort.

'So you're going to kill me, if you've got the guts to kill a man in cold blood!'

'Twenty years breaking rocks gives a man guts to do anything, buddy. I survived because I thought every day about the time I'd face you sons of bitches and take my due! You'd better say your prayers, mister, because you're on your way to the badlands in the sky!'

'You talk too much, mister!'

Judd, who'd been watching for such a move, saw Jonas tense into a crouch and his hand snake out for his gun.

Judd smiled and laughed aloud as his own gun went off a fraction before Jonas's weapon fired. Judd saw the spread of blood seep across Jonas's chest like a crimson flower unfolding. He'd had to goad Jonas into going for his gun. Judd knew he could never have deliberately killed the man in cold blood. He needed the draw to activate his reflex, but now the goal he'd waited and prayed for was achieved. Jonas Goodison was dead.

He holstered the Peacemaker, feeling strangely drained of strength. He looked about him, but the two gunshots had been ignored or even not heard.

He staggered away and returned to his mare. She nickered as he drew near. He patted her neck.

'It's OK, girl. We'll be riding out before too long.' He laid his head against her shoulder while he fought the feeling of inertia.

He was back to himself again when he heard the horsemen coming down the valley at a head-long gallop. Good old Ed. It sounded as if the whole of the range and the townsfolk of Sweetwater had turned out.

He mounted up and met them at the gates of the ranch. He held up his arm to Ed, who was riding in front of the bunch of men coming behind him. Dawn was now breaking, the moonlight fading. Ed surveyed the homestead before saying tersely:

'Everything's quiet. Anyone home or are they out on a raid?'

Judd laughed.

'You won't believe this but I witnessed a drunken orgy that would never have happened if Luke had been alive! They're all there waiting, like lambs to the slaughter! The battle's half-won already!'

But it wasn't going to be as easy as that. The sounds of many horsemen roused the sleeping men in the barn. A yell and a gunshot brought them all awake, bleary-eyed but reaching for their guns out of habit.

There was an outpouring of men from the barn, which brought a response from the crew in the bunkhouse. As Judd and Ed Summers and his men swept into the yard they galloped into a hail of slugs fired wildly and mostly into the air.

Judd felt the hiss of a bullet as he crouched low over the mare's neck, aiming for a *pistolero* who was only partly dressed.

He heard the boom of an explosion. The shock waves shook the ground. Dimly he knew that the barn had blown up. He reached the ranch house; his aim was to find Buster Goodison. Rage against Buster filled the void left by the death of Jonas. This was a new kind of rage, not for what happened to himself but for what had happened to Milly. It was the first time he'd ever fought for another person. In the past, it had always been for himself.

There was no one in the Goodison living-quarters except the half-dressed house-keeper, looking drunken and bemused.

'Where is he? Where's Buster Goodison?' he barked at her, grabbing her by the throat. She stared at him, glassy-eyed.

'Who're you?' she managed to mutter.

'It don't matter who I am. Where's Buster?'

137

She giggled stupidly.

'Where else? The son of a bitch sloped off to that Indian slut he keeps in the line cabin on the north range. He went off when the boys got out of hand. It's our little secret, even Jonas doesn't know about her! Don't tell him I told you, or he'll kill me!'

Judd shoved her down hard on her truckle bed and turned to leave. North. So the bastard had ridden north. He could follow his tracks and surprise the son of a bitch.

SEVEN

Milly thought long and hard as she rode away to go home and reassure her father that she was OK. He would be worrying about her long absence. Even out on the range, working with the men, she'd always come home at night. But the urge to be there with Ed Summers and the rest of the ranchers and help to give Buster Goodison his come-uppance was too hard to resist. A man who could kill his own brother and kidnap and try to rape her was a rat, and she would take great pleasure in seeing him lynched. Shooting would be too good for him.

So, determined, she rode on towards the Lazy S ranch. In the far far distance, on the horizon, she saw a haze of what she took to be a black cloud. There was a storm brewing. Little did she know it was the smoke from her own father's ranch.

It took longer than she expected to find Ed Summers' tracks. She was now well into unfamiliar country. She was riding blind now, for some of the tracks could have been from the Goodisons' own men when out working the range.

Then she saw the lone rider. Her heart leapt as she recognized the broad shoulders and the way he tilted his head. It was Judd, and all the fury and resentment of his ordering her to remain with Ed's wife overcame her real feelings. Fearlessly she rode towards him.

He was watching her incredulously, his face dark with anger.

'What in hell are you doing out here?' he barked at her.

She drew her head up proudly.

'I'm looking for Ed. I want to be in at the kill!'

'Too late. They're at it now. Mopping up, most like. Now you just turn your horse around and get the hell back to Ed's place!'

'Don't you dare to speak to me like that! I want to see Buster Goodison lynched!'

'Well, you're out of luck! I shot him. He's lying back there near a line cabin.'

'What was he doing there?'

Judd gave her a quizzical glance; his eyes suddenly twinkled.

'He kept a woman there for his own personal use, if you know what I mean!'

'A woman? What woman?'

'A squaw. An outcast of her tribe, I suspect. So just set your butt for home and I'll escort you there for fear any of Goodisons' men got away. They'll not deal kindly with you if you're caught!'

She looked at him mutinously.

'Why aren't you there helping with the mopping up? Is it that you'd rather face a man one to one rather than face a gun battle?'

He laughed easily.

'Lady, you don't faze me. If you're trying to anger me, you'll have to insult me all day! I'm confident in myself in all situations but I don't put my neck out for other folk's problems. What Ed Summers and his men do is no concern of mine. I've done what I set out to do and that's it!'

'If I ride with you, will you face my father?'

He shrugged. 'Why should I? It all happened a long time ago and he's living through his own punishment. I reckon a man should only suffer so much. I'll escort you home and then I'll ride on.'

Milly felt a stab of disappointment.

'My father would want to thank you for

saving me.'

'I'll take it as said. Now should we make for your ranch?'

They cut across country and Milly showed the way through a narrow pass used in the old days by Indians to get from one range to another. They camped and rested their horses in a stand of trees. Once again, Judd sniffed that fresh pine smell of freedom. He knew he would never ever forget the stink of prison life, that the scent of pine forests would always remind him of those other smells.

He spoke little as they camped and crouched around the small fire, sharing Judd's rations. To Milly he seemed morose and unbending. She little dreamed he was thinking of the past and how much he had missed in life.

The mare whinnied. Suddenly Judd was alert to what was going on around him. Milly saw the way his gun jumped into his hand on reflex.

'What is it?' She was ashamed at the

tremor in her voice.

'Be quiet!' His tone was brusque and impatient. She fought down the feeling of outrage that he should speak to her so ... so ... ungentlemanly, and the word in her mind startled her. When was the last time she'd thought of that word? She'd never thought of any of the hands she worked with as gentlemanly! They were just cowpokes. She held her breath and waited and watched Judd crawl away using the lush undergrowth as cover.

Then with a mounting horror, she saw a man move into the clearing leading a lame horse. He had a rough bandage around his head. So, she reckoned, he was one of Goodison's men. He was moving cautiously, horse reins in one hand and his gun waving around unsteadily in the other.

Then Judd burst out of the thicket, gun firing. His first bullet took the horse in the chest, the second, as the stranger's gun exploded, slammed the stranger in the forehead. He spun round and collapsed on to the ground.

Then Judd looked at Milly.

'You see what you could have faced all alone? You're a fool woman, you know!' He coolly uncocked the Peacemaker before thrusting it back in its holster.

'What should we do about him?' Milly stared down at the corpse.

'We've no time to worry about him. I'd better look at the horse.' He turned away. Milly thought what a cold-hearted bastard Judd was.

But she saw Judd's more tender side. He crouched down, ran a gentle hand over the horse's head and saw the faintest of quivers. The animal was not yet dead. So Judd rose to his feet, drew his gun and shot the beast in the head. Then he turned to Milly.

'Let's get out of here before the shots attract anyone else who got away from the Lazy S.'

They rode in silence and by nightfall came within sight of Jim Burke's range. They were both conscious of the smell of smoke in the air. It grew stronger as they approached the homestead. Then Judd said softly:

'I want you to wait here while I go and take a look-see, so don't argue but wait until I come back!'

She looked at him with frightened eyes.

'Why? Do you think something's happened? It could only be that the boys are logging and burning up branches...' her voice trailed away as she saw his grim expression. He cursed inwardly. If the fool woman hadn't ignored his order to remain at the Summers' ranch, he wouldn't have to tell her what he already suspected.

'I think it's more than that,' he said gruffly. 'Now just you wait here until I come back!' With that he scrambled up the incline. He took his spyglass and raked the land below.

It was as he suspected. He saw the blackened remains of buildings surrounding what was left of the main house. The scene reminded him of the devastation he'd seen as a boy with his father after an Indian raid on a stopping place for stagecoaches. The same blackened charred skeletons of cabins with smoke still rising lazily into the air.

He could see no movement anywhere. No humans, no horses. He saw that the corral fences were broken down as if panicked animals had charged them and fled. Then his spyglass caught and held on to a lone object in the yard in front of the smouldering ranch house. It couldn't be ... but it was. It was Jim Burke's clumsy contraption that was a wheelchair and there was a figure in it!

He watched intently for any sign of movement. Move, damn you, he muttered to himself. For the love of God, I don't have to confront her with his dead body! But there was no movement.

Hastily, he joined her down below, stones and dirt tumbling down with him. He saw her anxiously watching him.

'Well?'

He saw her lips quivering.

'Not good. I may as well tell you now. Goodison must have ridden on to the ranch after you got away.' He hesitated and then said softly, 'I'm sorry, Milly, but he fired the whole homestead!'

She gave a little scream of protest and covered her mouth with her hand.

'Oh, God! What about Father?'

Judd didn't answer. He couldn't. There were some things a man couldn't do and one of them was to tell a woman he was coming to care for that her father could be dead, all alone, surrounded by the burned-out shell of his spread.

He watched the conflicting emotions flit across her face and he had never admired her more. She might be a stubborn bitch, but by God, she had guts!

At last she sat up, stiff and proud on her mount. Lifting her chin she said quietly:

'Well? What are we waiting for? Let's go and see what the bastard's done, shall we?'

Carefully they picked their way down into the valley below. Milly could see for herself the tiny blobs of black become the burned-out shells of the barns, the stables, the bunkhouse and the blacksmith's shop, even the soddy built half underground as a cold chamber had been fired. Then her eyes raked what had once been a sprawling ranch house. She couldn't keep back the tears.

Judd waited. She still hadn't picked out that lone chair...

Then she saw it and gave a great cry. Spurring the tired horse she began a headlong gallop. He followed, his heart heavy. He knew what to expect. Buster Goodison wouldn't leave Jim Burke alive to bear witness against him.

But when he dismounted beside Milly and joined her as she bent over her father, he realized that Buster Goodison hadn't killed Jim Burke. There were no bullet wounds.

Instinctively he put an arm about her. She didn't pull away but just stared at the slumped figure.

'Milly ... please ... let me look at him. I think he had a seizure.'

Her head turned towards him and she buried it into his shoulder.

'Oh God! I should never have left him! I

should have been with him when they came!'

'It's not your fault, Milly! Brace yourself, girl! He went quickly. Better that way than shot by Buster and the mob!'

Milly wrenched herself away from Judd and turned on him.

'It's all right for you to say brace yourself! It's my father lying there! You couldn't possibly understand!'

Judd looked at her and their eyes, hers stormy and full of tears, locked together, then she realized what she'd said and her hand came up to her mouth.

'Judd, I'm sorry. I forgot.'

'Yes, well, it happened a long time ago. We'll forget it, shall we?'

Embarrassed, she looked around at the devastation, then she gave a great cry.

'There's no one about! They must have killed everyone! Annie! Where's Annie and the rest of the men?' The moment of embarrassment passed in this greater worry.

'Milly, stay with your father and I'll take a

look around.'

Judd didn't wait for an answer and Milly, shivering uncontrollably, sank down by the wheelchair, her head propped on her dead father's knees.

It didn't take long to discover the charred remains in the barn. He stepped into still-smouldering charcoal and saw that there were five bodies. One of them had been a woman.

He returned to Milly, his face muscles tight. She didn't have to ask the crucial question. He couldn't bring himself to look at her as he said quietly:

'I'm sorry, Milly ... they're all dead!'

'And Annie? Did they take her away?'

He shook his head.

'No!'

Milly broke down and cried as she'd not done since she was a child.

Judd let her cry. There was no one but himself to see the self-contained Milly Burke cry and it would be their secret.

While she grieved for her father and Annie

and the rest of the men, he carefully removed the bodies. Because there was no shovel at hand he scooped two shallow indentations in the hard ground with his hands, placed the bodies in them and covered them over with rocks, to protect the corpses from wild animals. Later, the bodies would be reburied properly according to Milly's wishes.

Then he came to her sitting by the wheelchair.

'Come, Milly, it's time to go. I'll take you to Ed Summers' place. Sally will look after you.'

Without a word she rose and went to stand beside the two mounds. For a long moment she meditated, then she said softly:

'I'll not forget either of you, and Pa, I promise I'll make the ranch prosper again and I'll keep up the good reputation of our horses. I won't let your work go for nothing! I'll build again, you'll see, and nobody but nobody will take it away from me! I swear it!'

Then she turned and went to the waiting Judd who was holding her mount. He helped to swing her aboard, then mounted up himself. They rode away towards Ed Summers' place.

EIGHT

Milly walked slowly away from the freshly dug grave situated under the small stand of trees not far from the original homestead. It had been a day she'd been dreading. She was last to leave the site. Some day, when the new buildings went up, there would be white-painted railings around the small plot designated as the cemetery. Now, her father lay there, flanked by Annie, and beyond them there were the four graves of the men who'd worked for her. She expected to lie there herself some day.

The townsfolk had been good in rallying around, as were the small ranchers, but now everyone wanted to get back to their own affairs. She was still staying with Ed Summers and his family but knew that the time had come to move out.

She ached to get back on to her own land.

She watched the horsemen ride away, and the buggies with the ladies of the community. There had been a hasty picnic while waiting for the travelling preacher to arrive to take the prayers. Now he had been long gone. The mourners had stayed long enough to talk and reminisce about Jim Burke, standing around the graves, but now she was glad to be alone.

She had searched the crowd for a glimpse of Judd but he had not shown up. She'd not seen him since he'd brought her back to Ed Summers' wife.

Thinking of him, she remembered how she'd broken down and wept and how gentle he'd been with her. She was disappointed that he'd not thought it important enough to come to the funerals after all he'd done for her. Yet he was still in town. The gunsmith's wife, who was the local gossip, had told her he'd taken a room in the widow Chorley's rooming-house. Why should he stay in Sweetwater, when he'd said his coming had to do with the Goodisons, and now they were dead, unless of course he meant to go after Judge Gannon again.

That thought gave her a cold feeling in her stomach. After all, Matthew Judd was an ex-jailbird and a killer. His years in the pen must have developed brutish instincts ... and yet, she had seen his gentle side. She became angry with herself. Why think of a complex man like Matthew Judd? She wasn't ever going to get involved with a man ever again. She'd made that vow when the news came that her fiancé, Steve, had been killed during the war.

She would live her life as she had done for the last ten years and to hell with men, Matthew Judd in particular.

But she needed help. She needed a new crew. Her father's prize horses were running wild on the range and there were cattle to be sorted and calves branded, and most important, she needed a new house before the winter set in.

She needed a man who could supervise all these problems.

She walked away from the fresh mounds of earth and returned to the rough shelter that one of Ed Summers' men had built for her. It was a tepee, the frame of supple willow branches covered by the tarpaulin that usually protected the goods on a long-haul wagon.

She'd salvaged a few kitchen appliances and made a bed of ferns laid in pine boughs. Sally Summers had given her a couple of blankets and a coffee-pot and a frying-pan, some flour and salt and a side of bacon. It would do her until she could move into her new home.

But she must round up some of the better horses and sell them. She knew her father never believed in keeping money in the bank. Too many hazards in banks. His own private stash of cash had been burned in the fire.

Now she had land, no buildings and the

only cash she could raise would be from the horses. But there had been a surprise when she'd mentioned all this to Ed Summers. It seemed that all the small ranchers who'd been done out of their land by the Goodisons were now too busy putting in claims to recover their property, and the Goodisons' own land was now being parcelled off to other would-be buyers. Disputes between newcomers and townspeople were rife. Nobody had time to help Milly with her building projects or the rounding up of her cattle and horses.

Milly felt bitter, remembering how her father had always helped those in need.

She felt helpless and alone. It was a new feeling for her, who had once commanded and bullied her father's crew. It was late fall; soon it would be winter and the snows would come.

She was crouched over her small fire, waiting for the coffee-pot to boil. She had fried bacon, the smell rising in the fresh pine air and was now mixing dough for panbread. A voice behind her said quietly:

'That smells good. Any chance of sharing that grub with me?'

She turned swiftly and toppled to her knees as she looked up at Judd towering over her.

'Steady,' he said, 'I didn't mean to frighten you.' He reached out a hand and helped her to rise.

She pulled sharply away from him.

'I'm not frightened! It was just that I wasn't expecting anyone around. Of course you can eat with me. I'll just make some extra panbread.'

He squatted down opposite her and she crouched again to go on with her dough-making.

She'd rolled her shirt sleeves up. In spite of himself he admired her smooth rounded arms and wondered what it would be like to have her close beside him in bed, her arms about him.

He scowled. Thinking thoughts like that got a feller nowhere and only caused trouble. Why should he think of an ornery bitch like her? God in heaven, there were women galore who were better-looking and more than willing to oblige. He must be going loco in the head!

She saw the scowl and wondered at it. Why come out here if he felt angry? Why come anyway?

She gave him a plate loaded with bacon and bread.

'Sorry, you'll have to eat with your fingers. I'm kind of short on forks.' She ate her own food out of the pan.

For a while they ate in silence. Later they shared the same tin mug to drink coffee. That seemed to bring them together, and eventually Milly asked aggressively:

'Why did you come here? I thought you were leaving this part of the country. Are you going after the judge? He's an old man, you know.'

'You wouldn't approve if I did?'

'Would it matter if I did or didn't? After all, you said it was your personal problem.'

'True. For years I've classed him with the

Goodisons, but lately I've grown tired of thoughts of revenge. Now the Goodisons are gone I feel … I don't know … as if a weight has been lifted off me. As for the old man … his time is nearly over. Maybe his conscience is enough punishment for him.'

'So why are you here?'

Judd hesitated for a while, looking into the small fire. Milly studied the weather-worn face, the grooved lines about his eyes and mouth. It was a strong face, which had known much suffering. The hard set of the lips, the turn of the nostrils, stirred her profoundly. Both of them had suffered at the Goodisons' hands.

The blue eyes looked darker, pain-ridden.

'I've no roots. I'm a drifter because of those bastards,' he said with some bitterness. 'I was ready to ride on to nowhere in particular and it came to me that wherever I was, I was just marking time until I moved on to … nowhere. Then I heard the talk in the saloon about the trouble the Goodisons' land was causing. That everyone wanted to be in on staking out some of their land. I thought of you. I wondered how you would get this place up and running again ... a lone woman...'

Milly's head reared up proudly. 'You can forget the lone woman business,' she said sharply. 'I don't need patronizing because I'm female! I'm not asking for help! I'll manage somehow!'

'Hold your horses, you all-fired female as you call yourself! Goddammit! Stop being so touchy! The fact remains you can't live in this tepee all winter!'

'Why not? Indians do! I can cover the tarpaulin with branches of pine later on and put another tarpaulin over it! It could be quite cosy.' Her voice trailed away at the quizzical look in his eyes. Then her eyes flashed and she spat at him,

'You're a son of a bitch, d'you know that? I was feeling quite confident until you came along and started pointing things out!' She knew he knew she was lying.

'Oh, come on now, let's stop arguing. I'm

here offering my help if you want it. I told you, I'm a drifter, so I might as well stay over the winter and help get this place into shape.'

Milly stared at him, suspicious, looking for a motive. She remembered her father's words when he first set eyes on him. *He's dangerous, Milly. He's bad medicine, so stay clear of him, Milly. That's an order!*

'Why do you want to help me? Just to make me feel bad that my father shot yours?'

Judd's eyes lifted heavenwards and he groaned.

'How many times do I have to tell you to forget all that? It's old history! Tell me, Milly, how do you propose bringing in those horses of yours and the cattle that're roaming all over your range? And how do you know how many of your calves are being branded as mavericks by other ranchers? How much stock will you have come spring?'

Milly got up from the fire and walked away. Judd watched the drooping shoulders and bent head. Milly Burke was going through a depth of humiliation she'd never ever imagined, and Judd's heart ached for her.

She came to a decision. She came back to the fire and he watched the expressive face harden as she took courage to face him and admit she needed help.

'If you want to stay and help me, I can't pay you in cash. Pa never kept cash in the bank. All I have is the land and the stock. You could pick out several horses for your own and some of the cattle. They'll bring good prices if we can round them up.'

'I'm not worried about the cash. I still have most of the prize money from the rodeo. All I want is food and a bed. Is it a deal?'

He held out his hand to her. She took it and shook it. The deal was struck.

'So I can regard you as my foreman?'

'Yes,' he said lightly, 'if you want to give me my proper title. The first thing I'll do is round up a few fellers I met in the saloon. We'll have some trees cut down, taken to the sawmill and sawn up into planks. I reckon a small one-room cabin would do to start with. We can always add to it as time goes by.'

'We?'

He smiled.

'You don't reckon I'm going to move on the minute the cabin's built do you? There's the other buildings to put up and the stock to see to, to get this place paying its way again.'

She frowned.

'If you figure on taking over half the ranch, then forget it! If you've got something like that in mind, then just ride out right now and forget the whole thing!'

He rose to his feet, his face dark with anger. His hand came up as if to strike her. She drew back, suddenly terrified, and watched while his eyes glittered savagely and he battled to control himself. His face eventually whitened; he was trembling as he turned and walked away towards the small cemetery, without a word being spoken.

Milly felt shame but the words had been said. She still didn't trust him. How could she when her father had warned her against him?

She'd built up the fire again, filled the

coffee-pot and set it on a log, and cleaned the mug and the plate and the frying-pan before he returned.

He stood before her, cool and remote, looking down at her from his great height.

'It's your shout, Milly. I'll stay if you want me. If you don't, I'm riding out right now!' He pushed his hat up above his forehead and waited. She stood quiet and still.

It was a deadlock.

Then, impatient and not liking Milly's stillness, he turned away and walked over to his mare. With a bound he was in the saddle. Then he eased the mare to the fire and raised his hat to her.

'Goodbye, Milly, you won't see me again. I'm sorry. I only wanted to help.' He swung on the reins, the mare turned sharply and began trotting away.

It was then that Milly came to life. He was actually going!

'Wait!' she called, but he kept on going. 'Wait!' she screamed, 'Please, stop! I'm sorry I said what I did! I really need your help!'

She saw with relief the horse slacken her stride, then she turned and Judd trotted back to her.

He didn't dismount, but sat and stared at her.

'What did you say? I didn't hear clearly.'

She took a deep breath. The bastard was putting her through her paces, like he was breaking in an unruly colt.

'I'm sorry,' she said between gritted teeth. 'I need your help. I shouldn't have said what I did!'

'You shouldn't have even thought it! By rights I should tan your ass, but because you're a lady I can't do that!'

'You once said I was no lady!'

His eyes gleamed.

'Does that mean I should tan your ass?'

She looked shocked.

'If you were a gentleman, you wouldn't make a statement like that,' she flared, showing some of her real spirit.

He laughed. 'Lady, I've never been accused of being a gentleman in my life!' Then his tone became grim again. 'Now, let's stop arguing. It gets us nowhere. You need my help and I'm offering it, with no strings attached. From now on you're strictly my boss. You pay me with stock and when this ranch of yours is up and running, I'll be on my way. Settled?'

She nodded.

'Thank you. I'm sorry—'

'Forget it. Where do I sleep tonight?'

She looked helplessly around, her eyes avoiding the tepee. He laughed again.

'I'm not suggesting sleeping in the tepee. Far from it. Do I sleep within calling distance of you, or should I respect your ladylike wishes to be far away and out of hearing? You might make unladylike noises through the night!'

She actually blushed. He was amused but though his lips quivered he managed to keep a straight face.

'I … er … maybe you should bed down under those trees over there.' She pointed to a small stand of trees which Judd planned to chop down later when building the cabin.

'Right. I'll just go and get my gear and settle the mare close by. She'll nicker if any wild cats come by. You not afraid of wild cats, Miss Milly?'

She gulped and bit her lip.

'No,' she lied. 'I can cope.' It was a snappy reply.

He grinned as he slowly moved off to untether the mare and lead her into the stand of trees. Let the ornery bitch sweat a little! She was a right stubborn, goddamned, uppity big-mouthed, spinsterish shrew, and he was amazed at himself for putting up with her. He should have just ridden on and ignored that shout to wait. He must be loco! He could still turn round and tell her to go to hell and ride out … but then if he did, he would be on that path to nowhere. At least she made life interesting. He had to keep his wits sharp to battle with her.

He reached for his bedroll and chose a tree with a hollow underneath it for his campsite. Then he heaved off the saddle and placed it for his head. He'd spent many nights in just such a situation. Tonight would be different. He would sleep well.

Reaching into his saddle-bags he took out a small bag of corn and hand-fed the mare, who nuzzled his arm. Then, when she was finished, he walked her down to the stream and ran his hand down her fetlocks while she drank.

Milly watched from her tepee. Every move with the horse was of gentle concern. He must love that mare very much. The thought comforted her. She laid herself down on her makeshift bed, and trusting her instincts went instantly to sleep.

It was daylight when she awoke to the smell of coffee. She sat up with a start, thrusting back her blankets. She yawned and stretched, then her mind cleared and she remembered Judd.

She saw him outside the tepee, crouched by the fire with hands outstretched to the blaze. He turned to her as she approached.

'Slept well?'

'Perfectly, thank you, and you?'

'Fine. I can sleep on a clothes'-line. I did that once, back in Tennessee. Got drunk in a saloon and it cost a couple of cents to hang over a lariat rope and sleep with the drunks. That rope must have been a good money-spinner for the barman. Still, it was better than sleeping on soggy ground during a rainstorm!'

'Did you really do that?' Milly found herself drawn to him and it was fascinating listening to him. She'd heard of line-sleepers but never really believed the tales about them.

'Only once when I was young just after my father…' he hesitated and then went on, 'died. I was pretty green and some guy got me drunk. When I woke up next morning I found myself facing the ground and the rope cutting into my chest. My pockets had been turned out and I hadn't a dime in the world.'

'Then what did you do?'

'I was violently sick and went and dunked myself into the creek. I spent the day either huddled under a tree or rushing into the bushes!'

Milly found herself laughing.

'That must have been a lesson for you! I bet you watched your back after that!'

Judd pulled a face.

'Not much of a lesson, I'm afraid. It was only months after that, that I took the rap for the bank robbery the Goodisons pulled. Jonas stashed a wad of cash on me after I was knocked out. I recognized his laughter. He and Luke got away with it by bribing the judge and I went down for their crime.'

Milly bit her lip. She was beginning to understand this outwardly cold man. Inside, a fire still raged.

'I'm sorry. They robbed you of the best part of your life.'

'At least I'm out and the rest of my life will be how I make it! Now, what about breakfast?'

They ate in silence and when they were finished, Judd said abruptly:

'I'm going into town to rustle up some

help. One of the first things we do is round up some of your horses. I'll cast around and see if there are any buyers in town. Do you want to come along and gather up some food staples? I reckon we need at least four men and they'll want feeding.'

'Good men will be hard to find. Everyone's gone mad wanting a piece of the Goodison ranch. I doubt whether you'll find anyone willing to help us.'

'I have my methods,' Judd said grimly. 'I earmarked several men in the saloon. I aim to *tell* them they're working for us, not ask.' He smiled at her. 'Don't worry. I'm not going to cause a ruckus, but you'll have a crew by tonight!'

So Milly tidied up the camp and Judd dowsed the fire and they set off on the trail to town. As they rode along, Milly wrestled with her conscience. She had a problem. She kept looking sideways at him until at last he said a little irritably:

'What's eating you, Miss Milly? You look as if you've been looking up a cow's behind!'

'Look, stop calling me Miss Milly! It's ridiculous, seeing as we're working together.'

'You're the boss. I aim to be respectful.'

'Talking about cows' behinds isn't being respectful. It's cow-hand talk between buddies. What's your name, Judd?'

'Matthew. Pa called me Matt, but I haven't been called anything but Judd for years.'

'I think I'll call you Matthew if you don't object?'

He shrugged.

'Call me what you like. I've been called many bad names in my time. I answer to anything. Now, what's your problem?'

She coughed.

'Matthew, I don't like to ask you … indeed, I wouldn't if it wasn't necessary, but–'

'For God's sake, spit it out! Whatever it is I'm not going to be shocked!'

'Then … then could you lend me ten dollars?'

He looked at her in surprise. That was the

last thing he'd had in mind.

'Ten dollars? Of course. I can lend you much more than that!'

She shook her head, still feeling too proud. She wouldn't have had to humiliate herself like this if her father had believed in banks.

'Ten dollars will be fine. All the ready cash Pa had went up in smoke.' She swallowed. 'The bank actually have the deeds and there's a loan, so I couldn't go asking for more cash. You understand? I've got to have cash for the storeman. Pa once accused Mr Riley of adding goods on to our bill that we hadn't taken. They had an argument about it and Mr Riley wouldn't let us put anything on the slate after that.'

'Look, I don't need explanations.' Jude drew out his roll of bills and peeled off a small wad. 'Here's fifty. I guess you'll be needing some feminine fal-lals as well. You can pay me back when you sell some horses.'

'Thank you.' Milly, very embarrassed but relieved, put the notes into her vest pocket. They rode on very quietly and then Milly looked at him sideways.

'You know, Matthew, you're a very understanding man and I appreciate what you're doing.'

Judd stared straight ahead as if he hadn't heard but inside he felt a warmth he'd never felt before. Milly might be an unbroken, untamed filly, but she was a mighty fine woman!

They found Sweetwater much quieter than usual. The men who knew Milly greeted her with eyes averted as if ashamed that they'd not rushed to help her in her need. Many of the townsfolk had experienced help from her and her father in the past. Now everyone was concerned with getting their share of the Goodison land.

It was a land rush all over again.

Judd noticed the lack of enthusiasm on the part of the townsfolk and it angered him. It was as if those same townsfolk were waiting for Milly to fail so that they could take over her land too. Greed seemed to be the all-important motive at this time.

He turned to her when they'd hitched their horses to a rail in front of the general store.

'I'll leave you here. I'm going to see if I can hire a wagon, if that's all right with you. I reckon we should stock up on hardware such as nails and axes and some other tools, if we're to start on that cabin. I'll be a couple of hours or so as I want to round up the men I had in mind.'

Milly nodded and bit her lip. What else could she do but agree?

NINE

The big man stood rocking on his heels as he gazed with blurry eyes at Judd. He was as tall and broad as Judd but not in good condition. His nose had been broken and he was an ugly sight, with a long matted beard streaked with grey and long straggly locks to match.

'I told you, mister, I'm the best bare-knuckle fighter in the west! I beat Rough-house Tyler in Chicago and Jimmy Black Kango in St Louis! I can still kick hell out of you, mister!'

'Then why don't you try? I'm willing to take you on!' Judd looked around at the gathering crowd of men. 'You heard him, fellers! He says he's the best. I say he ain't!'

There were shouts and whistles as the crowd saw that there was to be some enter-tainment. Judd turned again to the big man. 'Sam, let's make this interesting. If you win I'll buy you two bottles of whiskey. If I win, you come and work for Miss Milly. Right?'

Sam lowered his head in thought. The chance of two free bottles of whiskey was enticing. Besides, he wanted to show this loud-mouth that he could still fight and win.

'You're on!'

Both men stripped off their shirts and laid guns and holsters in two tidy piles. The crowd stepped back to give them room. Nobody wanted a big hefty feller flung on them.

Sam spat on his hands and went into a crouch. He growled and flung himself at Judd. Judd sidestepped, clipping Sam on the ear and the fight was on.

Milly spent some time in the general store and did some personal buying as well as getting the essentials. She wondered whether Judd had managed to hire a buggy or wagon. There was so much they needed to get a new start. Her father would have been devastated if he'd known what had happened. She also worried over the business of hiring new labour.

She heard cheering and whistling. Looking along the street she saw a crowd of men. By craning her neck she could see two tall men squaring up to each other. One of them looked like Judd.

She hurried along the sidewalk to watch, and was just in time to hear him propose a challenge. So, Judd considered one of his methods was to beat the daylights out of a man to recruit him! Milly reckoned that by the size of the man, maybe Judd had taken on more than he could manage. But she saw that she was wrong as she watched the short sharp encounter.

She found herself cheering Judd on as the men traded punches. She screamed when the stranger suddenly pulled a knife, but Judd was ready for rough-house tricks and twisted the man's wrist until he dropped the knife. Then, with a sudden jerk, Judd flung him over his back and the man went sprawling on to the ground. He groaned and tried to rise but fell back, winded.

'You want any more of the same, feller?' Judd panted as he bent over him, 'Or do you reckon I beat you fair and square?'

'I give up,' growled Sam. 'What do you want me to do?'

'I want you sober and ready to ride. Usual wages and food all found. From now on, you're working for Miss Milly. Right?'

'Right.'

Judd hauled Sam to his feet and dragged him over to the nearest horse trough. Taking him by the scruff of the neck he dunked the man into the water. Sam spluttered and struggled, but when he came up for air he looked at Judd with a new respect.

'Jesus H Christ! You didn't have to do that!' he said, shaking his straggly hair and cursing strongly.

'Just to show you who's boss. Here's a quarter. Go and get a shave and haircut and report to us in front of the general store in two hours. If you don't, I'll come looking for you and you'll wish you'd never been born!'

The man slunk away and the crowd dispersed. Judd went off down the street, not having seen Milly watching.

Judd's next stop was at the hostelry. He was looking for a young half-breed who'd cared for Judd's mare when he'd first come into town. His name was Joe Deerhunter and Judd had been impressed by his love of horses.

Now Joe listened to Judd's offer of work with horses. His boss would be the fiery woman rancher. He wasn't sure about working for a woman. He would have preferred working for the big man. Still, it was a good offer. Not many ranchers would take on a half-breed. He stuck out his hand and he and Judd struck a bargain.

Judd was pleased with his initial success. Now he would round up the old man who hung around the saloon doing all the dirty jobs that the bar-owner couldn't get his swamper to do, like keeping the latrines clean and carrying water and getting rid of kitchen waste after the butchering of a steer.

Old Ben was a short stringy feller, like a hunk of streaky bacon, Judd reckoned, but though he was near on sixty, he was wiry and could still do a full day's work. Ben looked surprised at Judd's offer.

'Me? Are you joking? You really want me to crew with you? I'm a has-been, so everyone says!'

'I don't. I reckon you only need a chance to show what you can do. It's up to you. If you want to, take a chance, or you can stay here up to your knees in beasts' entrails!'

Ben looked Judd up and down and then

rubbed his hairy chin.

'Then you're not pulling my leg. You're really hiring me?'

'Yes. You'll be working for Miss Milly. She needs all the help she can get.'

'Right. I'll pack my war bag and I'll be with you in less time than a skunk can fart!'

'Meet us in front of the general store in two hours.'

The fourth man Judd had in mind would take more persuasion. He was the man who had an old Conestoga wagon. If Judd played his cards right, he could hire the man and the wagon would come with him, and so save having to spend more cash on hiring.

The Conestoga wagon was huge as Judd remembered it: an old prairie wagon from way back in the early days when men first came out West. If all went well he could take back a whole mess of equipment that would be needed for the building of the cabin and a small bunkhouse. He reckoned Milly would go off in one of her flouncy prideful fits but what the hell ... he had the cash, why not make life easier for them all?

She could rant and rave but she'd come round in the end.

He made his way to a small cabin a little out of town. Dan Emery was a saloon regular and Judd had watched him when he'd first arrived in town. He was a man shunned by his neighbours. He drank alone and at a given time would stumble out of the saloon and go home. He had no wife and as far as Judd knew, no relatives.

They'd talked and Judd found that once started, Dan Emery couldn't stop. The loneliness of his life and a willing listener brought forth revelations he'd never expected to share with anyone. Very soon, Judd had known all about him, much more than any of Dan's neighbours had learned in years.

The man had been a prison warder, working in the fearsome Arkansas penitentiary. One night, during a prison breakout, two prisoners had killed Dan's wife and children after raping her. They were both caught and shot but it was too late for Dan and his family. Sick at heart, he'd left Arkansas to put the past behind him, but the memories had gone with him, turning him to drink for oblivion.

At first Judd had been repulsed by the man's profession, but soon, as he'd listened to the anguished babblings, he'd come to pity the man. Now, he reckoned, he might do this man a good turn by motivating him to work for a woman.

Dan was surprised to see him riding into his yard.

'Howdy!' he called, putting down his axe beside a pile of logs. 'What brings you here? I thought you would be long gone by now.'

'I've come to talk,' Judd said easily as he dismounted. He shook hands with Dan.

'Come inside. I've got coffee on the boil.'

Over coffee, Judd watched Dan for a reaction. Mornings were the best time to get through to this man. He watched while Dan raked around to find a half-empty bottle of rotgut whiskey. He saw the shadows playing over the man's face as he fumbled with the cork and took a swift drink before returning to his coffee.

'Well? What about it? It's time you did something with your life and put the past behind you. You've grieved long enough, Dan. You want company and fresh air and a kind of respect for yourself. How about it, Dan? You'd be doing Miss Milly a favour. She needs men at this time to get her spread up and running again. I know no better man to ramrod her place than you … and you can do it! Will you?'

Dan considered and took another drink of liquor.

'I don't know. I'm finished, Judd. I ain't got the heart. I'm dead inside. I still see the wife and kids … lying there…' His voice broke. 'Goddamn it!' he suddenly shouted and hurled his coffee-cup into the fireplace, shattering it into pieces.

Judd sat quite still. Then he said quietly:

'It's a nightmare, Dan. Outside in the big world, the nightmare will grow less. You need to be with others. Doing Miss Milly a favour could be a way of helping all womenfolk in distress. You'd want someone to help your wife if the situation had arisen?'

'But the situation did arise and no one was there, not even me, goddammit!'

'So, you can help someone else! Dan, take the first step and begin a new life!'

Tears trickled down Dan's face and he quickly wiped them away.

'OK. I'll do it for the woman's sake. God help me, I wouldn't like to see her fail and know I hadn't lifted a finger to help her!'

'Good.' Judd stood up. 'Thanks for the coffee. Oh, by the way, could you bring your wagon along? We're badly in need of transport. I've a load of barbed wire and tools and other stuff to take back. We're having to build again from scratch. You heard about the Goodisons firing the Burke ranch?'

'Yes, I heard something about it.' Dan rubbed a hand over his eyes. 'The bastards got their dues. I'll bring it along. Where do we meet?'

'In two hours in front of the general store.'

'Right. I'll be there.'

Judd rode away, heart lightened. When Dan got himself straightened out he would be a good man indeed to have around. Now he could concentrate on buying the list of things he had in mind.

Two hours later, the wagon, pulled by four dray-horses pulled up before the store. Already waiting were the other three recruits.

Milly, laden down with packages, walked the sidewalk slowly, wondering how successful Judd had been. She saw him talking to four men as the storeman and his helper were loading up a wagon with an assortment of goods.

She gasped. One was a youthful half-breed and the other three she knew as the town's drunks!

Judd saw her, smiled and came to her to relieve her of the heaviest parcels.

'I see you've spent your time well.' He grinned, then his face hardened when she said furiously:

'What in hell are you doing with those

men? They're riff-raff!'

'They're your new crew, Milly. You're their new boss!'

'Like hell I am! Get rid of them at once!'

His chin lifted and his jaw tightened as he said softly:

'If they go, I go! It's your choice!'

They glared at each other, then Milly's eyes dropped. Judd had won.

TEN

Milly was supervising the coming Fourth of July celebrations. A whole year had gone by, and though the preparations wouldn't be on the scale loved by her father, she was proud of what she and Judd and her men were achieving.

There would be no flags or bunting and the arena was to be the corral usually kept for mares and foals. She had never dreamed that one year on they would be in a position to hold the traditional celebration, but during the last months when townsfolk and ranchers saw how she fought hard to keep the ranch going, they'd asked and begged her to keep up the tradition. The pressure had been too much and now they were actually putting the last touches, ready for the big day.

It had been a traumatic year. The men she hadn't approved of had surprised her. They and Judd had made the soddy that had once been a cold store into a temporary bunkhouse. Half burnt, it had been a shell; they'd reroofed it with turf after putting in new timbers. Though they'd lived rough, none had complained.

Her small cabin had been finished in double-quick time, as had a cookhouse close by which served both her, in the cabin, and the men in the soddy. It had all been a race against the coming of winter.

There had been a sustained round-up of both cattle and horses, which had taken weeks, combing the hills and draws to bring them all down into the valley before the storms began.

The best horses and some of the cattle had gone to the buyers and the cash was a godsend. It had enabled Milly to lay in stocks of dried foods to last over the winter.

Christmas had been a dreary round of feeding and caring for horses on the poor stock of hay they'd managed to save. She'd spent her time in roasting huge rounds of meat, baking large batches of bread and doing all the chores poor Annie used to do. It was an eye-opener for her, for she'd never considered all the duties Annie had done, like feeding hens and suckling calves after milking the one cow they kept for domestic purposes, along with making butter, and cheese in a muslin bag.

Her one worry about Judd not staying had gradually died away. She leaned on him far more than she realized. Now, he was a permanent prop, or so she thought.

She looked about her as Joe Deerhunter reinforced part of the corral fence. He'd proved himself to be one of her most skilled workers. He could build a makeshift tepee in less time than it took a man to unpack his war bag, a great help if a mare was slow in foaling or a cow was having trouble calving. He also knew what roots and plants to look for for healing, all learned from his mother and her people. Now he looked at Milly and grinned.

'I don't think the wildest horse will get over that fence, Miss Milly. If the whole lot is surrounded by wagons it'll be as good as any proper arena. How many entrants do you think there'll be, Miss Milly?'

'Ten or twelve, maybe more. Maybe having to charge an entrance fee this year might put some folk off, but we couldn't have raised the prize money any other way.'

'Folk understand, Miss Milly. I heard fellers talking in the saloon that they'd rather pay than not have the contest.'

'Oh, good. I was feeling very guilty about charging but things aren't the same since Pa died.' She looked pensive. There were many days when Milly missed her father's presence. She would have given anything to hear his roaring bad-tempered voice.

Joe Deerhunter looked after her as she walked away towards her cabin, a lonely despondent figure. He sighed. He wished that Judd would make a move. Everyone could see he was silly about her and Joe couldn't understand why he didn't do something about it. Judd was hard to understand. He kept his feelings to himself.

Judd was bringing in a string of horses along with big Sam.

'Hi, there! Do you want to help pick out the best horse for the contest?' His voice rang out loudly. Both Joe and Milly looked over the remuda expertly. Milly quickened her stride and followed to the corral behind the cabin.

When they were all safely inside and milling about, Judd joined her at the rails.

'You look tired. Maybe you should take off for town and do things women do for a change.'

'Huh! Just like a man! You think I can leave

all the kitchen arrangements to Jessie, who's never cooked for hundreds of folk before?'

'Neither have you cooked for hundreds but you're coping and so can she.'

She looked at him consideringly.

'You want to get rid of me? Now why?'

He laughed. 'Must there be an ulterior motive? All I was worried about was you. I know you'll be thinking of your pa at this time. I don't like to see that droop to your lips!'

'Oh!' She was taken aback. During all these months he'd never given the slightest hint of being interested in her personally. He had worked for her and kept his distance. She'd paid him back the money she owed him and he'd taken it without protest. They had had a business arrangement and that was that.

Suddenly she felt shy, something she hadn't done in years, not since the days of her youth with her first love. She'd stifled that early interest in Judd in the task of getting the ranch up and running again. It had been a monumental task with no time for personal issues.

Now she panicked and snapped a reply which she regretted later.

'It's no business of yours how I look!' She left him hastily.

Judd stared after her, balefully. Right! That was it. After the rodeo he was packing his bags and he'd be on his way! He should have done it months ago. The bitch wasn't worth the effort of helping her! She was more man than woman. So to hell with her!

Enraged, he bawled at Sam and Joe to get a move on and stop scratching their asses. He stalked off to find his mare. He needed a quiet time to himself.

The next few days passed quickly. At last it was the Fourth of July and the wagons were coming in with families. Old friends of Jim Burke's came along to criticize and compare the old days with the new order of things. Contenders of the main contest were rolling in, some from neighbouring ranches and some itinerants who hoped to make a quick buck or get hired as the case might be.

The womenfolk had rallied round and brought their own specialities. Everyone looked around at the new buildings and tried to ignore the blackened sites that remained from the fire.

Everyone agreed that Milly and Judd and their men had done a fine job.

There was a new mayor of Sweetwater, a brash young man who was full of his own importance. He approached Milly and Judd who were welcoming the newcomers.

'Howdy, folks! You're putting on a great show here between you. There were bets in town that you'd never survive, Miss Milly, but you did, by God!' Then he said in a ringing tone so all could hear, 'And when will you be sending for the preacher, Miss Milly? I reckon he's a mite overdue!'

There was a shocked silence from those standing by and all eyes turned to Milly, but it was Judd who reacted.

Phil Ludlow never saw the punch that connected to his jaw but he felt it as he went down flat on his back. He struggled to lean on one elbow and shook his head, feeling his jaw.

'What in hell...?' But when he looked around, he was alone. Everyone had moved away and both Milly and Judd were heading for the corral, for the contest was about to begin.

Judd was quiet. He made no remark about the mayor's assumption but Milly knew by his expression he was furious. She wanted to say something but could not find the words.

They elbowed their way through the crowd and without a word, Judd lifted her on to the old Conestoga wagon along with Jessie. Then he left them, to go and judge the contest.

Milly watched the contestants with detached interest. In other years she'd found it exciting, had urged on the hopefuls and felt the pain of those unfortunates who were catapulted to the ground. Today she had personal things to think about.

Amidst the cheers and sighs as the contestants came and went she watched Judd as he helped to bring in the untamed, unridden animals. He was not riding today for which she was thankful.

She thought of the moment when he'd said he was worried about her. She'd been a fool to panic and snap at him. Nobody else in the world would ever worry about her. She was entirely alone and the thought was disturbing. Should she tell him how she felt? What did she feel, anyway? Milly was confused. Females didn't talk about their emotions to men not of their family. It was considered fast by the church members to even think about love. Love? The word startled her. How could she love a man whom, part of the time, she liked and the rest of the time she quarrelled with and disliked?

She mentally shook herself. This had come about all because he'd said he was worried about her and didn't like to see her lips droop! But try as she might, she couldn't get rid of her thoughts and concentrate on the contest. Damn all men and Judd in particular!

The contest was over. A young rider from a ranch near Frankfort, all bruised and bloody, had finally won the contest from all comers. He was grinning as he spat out a loose tooth and gave a rebel yell when Milly presented him with the prize money. He impulsively kissed her, leaving her with a bloody smudge on the cheek.

'Sorry, ma'am. Don't know what came over me! I'm sure pleased. This means I can marry my girl! Yippee!'

Then he leaped down into the crowd and she saw him making his way to the lines of beer-barrels beside the trestle-tables of food.

The party was about to begin.

She smiled at the young man's brash eagerness about his girl. She looked down at herself in her habitual garb of pants and shirt. It had been a long time since she'd worn petticoats and she recalled the uncomfortable restricting corset with distaste. It was far more comfortable wearing pants and shirt. But maybe she'd made a mistake. She should have shown her more feminine side to Matthew. Perhaps for the party she should go and change and titivate herself up a little.

She was on the way to her cabin when Judd approached her. He looked grim, as though in one of his dark moods. She looked apprehensively at him.

'What is it, Matthew?'

'I've just come to tell you I'm leaving. I'm sorry, Milly, but I reckon it's time I was on my way. The worst's over and Sam's a good man...'

'Leaving? But you can't leave, Matthew! I've grown used to you being around! This place won't be the same without you!'

He stared into the distance. He wasn't going to let her get to him. He'd made up his mind and that was that.

'I'm sorry, Milly. The longer I stay, the more your reputation will suffer. You heard what Ludlow said. Probably all Sweetwater thinks the same, so I'm going and that's it!'

'Matthew, please ... don't go. Look, I'll make over half the ranch to you, if you'll stay!' She hesitated and her heart started to thump. The words stuck in her throat but she managed to blurt out; 'I'll even marry you to make it all legal!'

'*Marry me?*' He gave a bitter laugh. 'If I ever marry, it'll be to a real woman! Not some female who wants to wear the pants and act like a man! Besides, as I said once before, I'm not interested in owning land. I'll not be bribed by marriage or the offer of land, Milly. You should know me by now!'

'I'm sorry ... I don't know what to say!' Milly fought back unaccustomed tears.

'No need to say a thing, Milly. We've done a lot of good things this last year as well as the bad things. We've argued and sometimes we've come near to hating each other. I could tell by your eyes when things got rough. I don't blame you. I'm a mighty hard man to understand. So this is goodbye, and good luck to you, Milly.' He touched his hat-brim, then gently nudged the mare with his spurs and they moved off.

Milly stood transfixed. For a moment she was paralysed with the suddenness of it all.

Then she screamed after him.

'Matthew! Don't go ... Matthew!' She began running after the horse and rider. He did not look back or even indicate he'd heard her cry. He was fast trotting out of hearing.

Then she saw the crowd around the beer-barrels open up and a very angry Phil Ludlow staggered towards Judd, waving a pistol in his hand. The drunken crowd had ribbed him unmercifully about getting a punch on the jaw from Judd and the jeers had whipped up the smouldering rage in him.

He watched as Judd cantered past him without glancing his way. Judd was too concerned over his last meeting with Milly to think about Ludlow. He was the least of his concerns.

Ludlow, full of his own importance as the new mayor of Sweetwater, took offence at Judd's ignoring him.

'Where the hell do you think you're going, Judd?' called Ludlow. 'Shouldn't you be sparking that woman of yours? It's your party, isn't it? You're the host. You should be there shaking a leg!'

Judd pulled up. He turned and trotted slowly back to Ludlow, who stood with legs apart, one hand hanging free and holding his gun firmly in the other.

'You trying to tell me something, mister?' Judd grated.

'Yeah. If you don't want the goods yourself, you shouldn't handle 'em!'

Slowly Judd slipped off the mare's back. He wrapped the reins around the pommel, smacked the mare on the rump and she trotted away.

'I think you should take those words right back before I stuff 'em down your throat!'

'Come and try, mister! You gave me a wallop when I wasn't looking for it. This time I'm all set!'

'Right! Drop your gun and I'll teach you a thing or two!'

Phil Ludlow's drunken laughter alerted the men around the beer-barrels that something was afoot. They liked nothing better than a good old rough-house and it looked likely to be one that they could talk about for years to come.

Both men threw their weapons into the dust. Ludlow put his head down and charged, arms flailing. Judd danced aside, clipping Ludlow under the ear. Ludlow staggered back and then came on with a roar of rage.

Catcalls and cheers filled the air, and Milly couldn't believe how quickly her guests' mood had changed. There was an underlying savagery amongst the men and their mood affected the two men now fighting.

Judd bared his teeth and waded in, his years of fighting to survive in the penitentiary keeping him cool. He knew all the dirty tricks a man was capable of. Phil Ludlow was a dirty fighter and his confidence had been boosted by many a saloon brawl but he soon found he'd met his match in Judd. The punches Judd took seemed to roll off him and he gave as good as he got. The two men sprawled in the dust, punching, gouging and biting, using every means to lay on the most punishment. Both men were bloody, knuckles raw and faces battered and bruised.

Every punch gave Judd an exhilarating sense of satisfaction. For months he'd lived under stress and now he'd found an outlet.

Phil Ludlow, his confidence shaken, found he had a desperate battle on his hands. He ducked and dived, wild punches either hitting or missing and yet Judd still came on like an all-powerful tornado.

Milly drew closer, the men watching giving her space and all she could do was to stand and watch.

Now both men were tiring. They staggered around and it was an effort to swing arms and connect with each other. Ludlow was gasping, his breath rattling in his throat, while Judd's mighty arms and shoulders, which had seen so much hard work breaking rocks, carried on regardless although his legs felt like jelly.

Then Judd managed a punch that con-nected to Ludlow's jaw and he was flung back to hit the ground as if catapulted from a horse. A universal sigh went up as Ludlow lay still.

Judd, swaying, watched him. The man didn't attempt to rise, so Judd bent, picked up his Peacemaker, holstered it and turned away, groggy and just about all in.

Then Milly screamed a warning and the men crowding round broke away. Judd turned just as Ludlow, who'd scrabbled for his gun raised it and took a shot at him. He took the slug in the shoulder instead of his back.

He rocked back on his heels, one hand up at his shoulder. As Ludlow tried to scramble to his feet, Judd drew the Peacemaker and using two hands to hold the heavy gun, shot Ludlow like a man who shoots a rat.

Then he took several swaying steps, dropped his gun and slid to his knees, head resting on his chest before keeling over.

Milly ran to him, crouching over him. He could barely see her for his senses were swimming. He managed to say in a faraway voice:

'They said you were better than the doc at

digging out bullets, now prove it!' He sighed and closed his eyes as he drifted in and out of consciousness.

'Damn you, Matthew Judd, don't dare to leave me now!' Milly cried in ringing tones, oblivious of the shocked crowd listening. He opened one eye, hearing her voice as at a great distance.

'I'm not going anywhere...' He closed his eyes again. She bent low over him as she tried to staunch the blood seeping from his wound with her neckerchief. She whispered in his ear:

'Listen to me, Matthew Judd, I swear before God, I'll never let you go again! I'll even stop wearing pants and wear skirts which I hate but I'll do it for you! You'll be the one to wear the pants in future!'

He opened his eyes wide and she was sure she saw a humorous twinkle in them.

'I'll sure hold you to that.' He groped for and held her hand before sinking down into overwhelming blackness. He never knew that big Sam carried him to the cabin or that Milly held his hand all the way, or that she cried as she dug out the bullet in his shoulder. It was more than two days before Judd regained his senses and found himself in Milly's bed and her asleep on a chair at the foot. He was swathed in bandages.

Then he remembered Milly's words and smiled. He'd hold her to her vow. He lay and watched her and saw the worry lines on her face. She'd lost weight. She looked vulnerable. How could he ever have thought she was more man than woman?

For him, lying watching her, she was all woman … his woman.

He couldn't wait to get up on his legs again. He'd show the ornery female who was boss but he'd break her in gently. He didn't hold with breaking a filly's spirit. It had to be done gradually. It made all the difference. That way you got a mare who'd follow you through thick and thin…

He smiled. From now on, life was going to be far more interesting! He lay back and slept.

The publishers hope that this book has given you enjoyable reading. Large Print Books are especially designed to be as easy to see and hold as possible. If you wish a complete list of our books please ask at your local library or write directly to:

Dales Large Print Books
Magna House, Long Preston,
Skipton, North Yorkshire.
BD23 4ND

This Large Print Book, for people
who cannot read normal print,
is published under the auspices of
THE ULVERSCROFT FOUNDATION

Roscommon County Library Service

WITHDRAWN
FROM STOCK

... we hope you have enjoyed this book.
Please think for a moment about those
who have worse eyesight than you ...
and are unable to even read or enjoy
Large Print without great difficulty.

You can help them by sending a
donation, large or small, to:

**The Ulverscroft Foundation,
1, The Green, Bradgate Road,
Anstey, Leicestershire, LE7 7FU,
England.**
or request a copy of our brochure for
more details.

The Foundation will use all donations
to assist those people who are visually
impaired and need special attention
with medical research, diagnosis
and treatment.

Thank you very much for your help.